STONE ARCH BOOKS
a capstone imprint

STONE ARCH BOOKS™
Published in 2014
A Capstone Imprint
1710 Roe Crest Drive
North Mankato, MN 56003
www.capstonepub.com

Originally published by DC Comics in the U.S. in single magazine form as Teen Titans GO! #1.

DC Comics
1700 Broadway, New York, NY 10019
A Warner Bros. Entertainment Company

Cataloging-in-Publication Data is available at the Library of Congress website:
ISBN: 978-1-4342-4789-6 (library binding)

Summary: Join Robin, Cyborg, Beast Boy, Starfire, and Raven as they battle for truth, justice, and pizza! In this adventure, the creepy kids from the HIVE Academy--Jinx, Gizmo, and Mammoth--have hacked into the Titans Tower game system, and the Titans get caught in a virtual reality gone mad!

STONE ARCH BOOKS
Ashley C. Andersen Zantop *Publisher*
Michael Dahl *Editorial Director*
Sean Tulien *Editor*
Heather Kindseth *Creative Director*
Alison Thiele *Designer*
Kathy McColley *Production Specialist*

DC COMICS
Kristy Quinn Original U.S. Editor

Printed in China by Nordica.
1013/CA21301918
092013 007744NORDS14

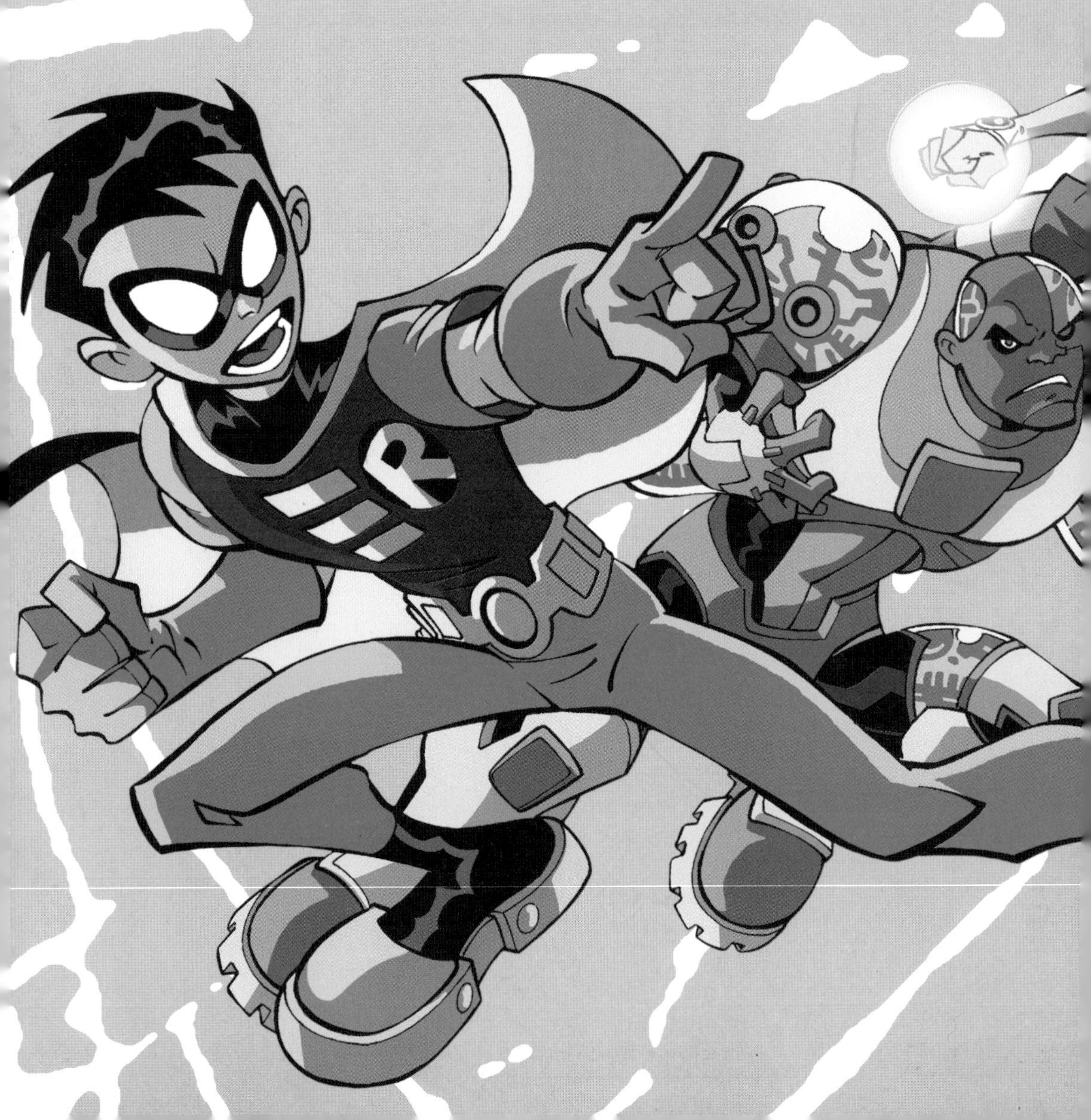

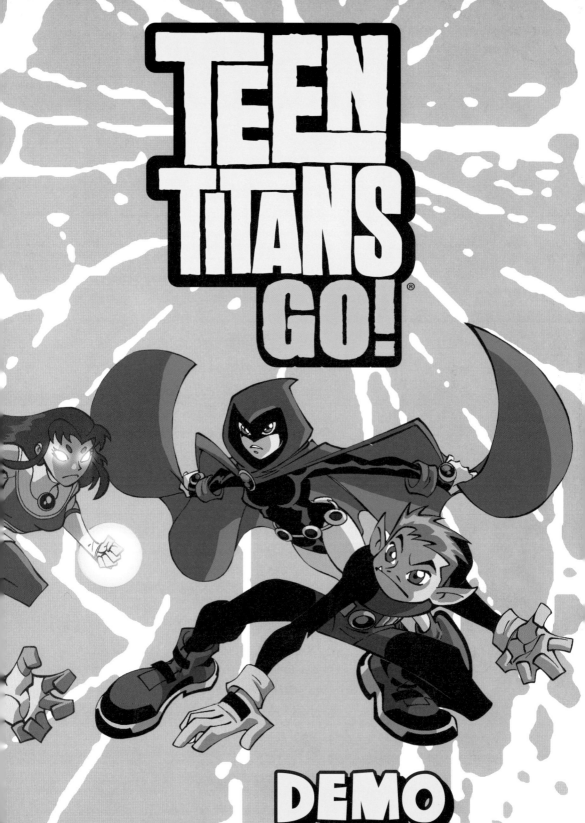

DEMO

J. Torres.. writer
Todd Nauck & Lary Stucker.....................artists
Brad Anderson.. colorist
Jared K. Fletcher.............................. letterer

TEEN TITANS GO!

ROBIN

REAL NAME: Dick Grayson

BIO: The perfectionist leader of the group has one main complaint about his teammates: the other Titans just won't do what he says. As the partner of Batman, Robin is a talented acrobat, martial artist, and hacker.

STARFIRE

REAL NAME: Princess Koriand'r

BIO: Formerly a warrior Princess of the now-destroyed planet Tamaran, Starfire found a new home on Earth, and a new family in the Teen Titans.

CYBORG

REAL NAME: Victor Stone

BIO: Cyborg is a laid-back half teen, half robot who's more interested in eating pizza and playing video games than fighting crime.

RAVEN

REAL NAME: Raven

BIO: Raven is an Azarathian empath who can teleport and control her "soul-self," which can fight physically as well as act as Raven's eyes and ears away from her body.

BEAST BOY

REAL NAME: Garfield Logan

BIO: Beast Boy is Cyborg's best bud. He's a slightly dim but lovable loafer who can transform into all sorts of animals [when he's not too busy eating burritos and watching TV]. He's also a vegetarian.

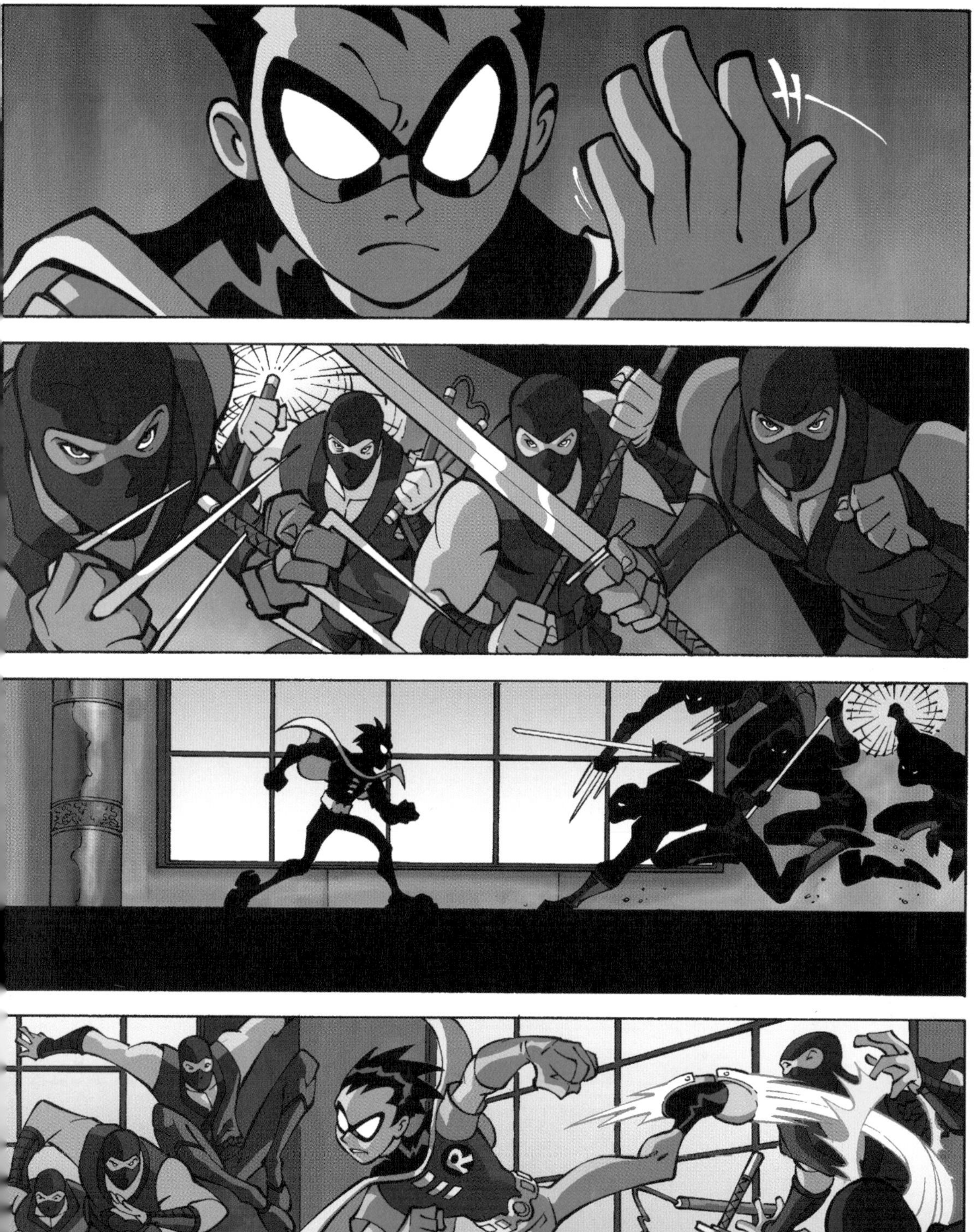

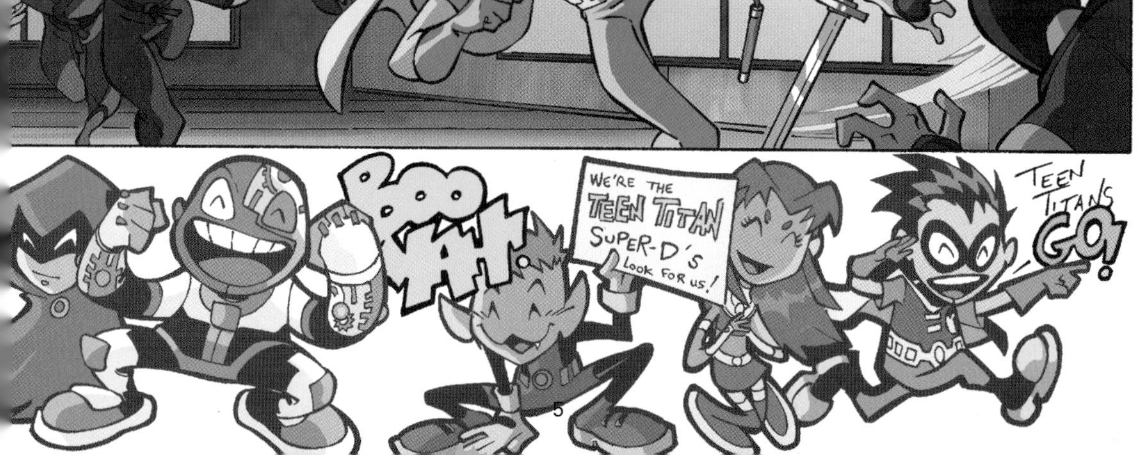
BOOYAH!
WE'RE THE TEEN TITAN SUPER-D'S Look for us!
TEEN TITANS GO!

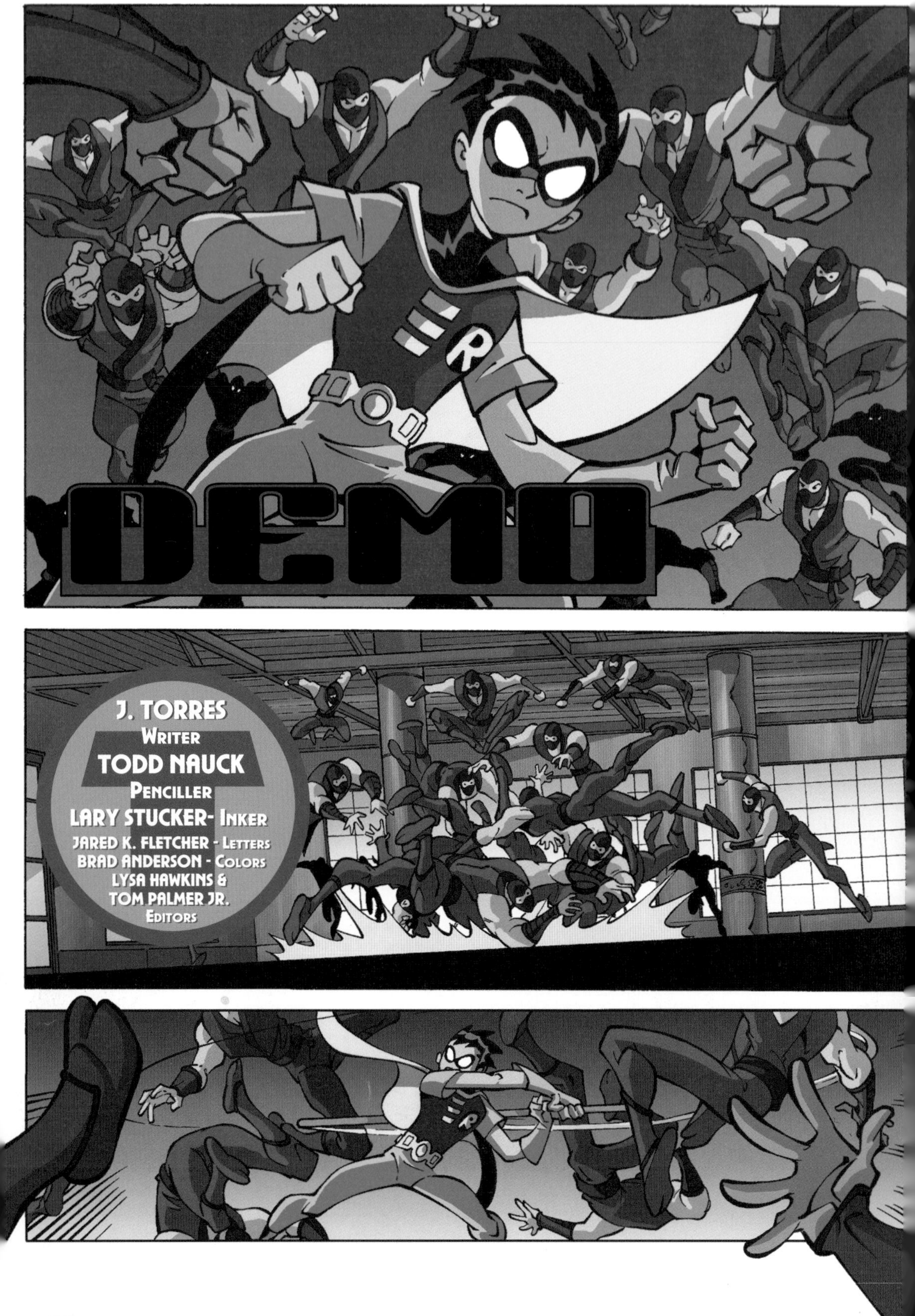
DEMO
J. TORRES
WRITER
TODD NAUCK
PENCILLER
LARY STUCKER- INKER
JARED K. FLETCHER - LETTERS
BRAD ANDERSON - COLORS
LYSA HAWKINS &
TOM PALMER JR.
EDITORS

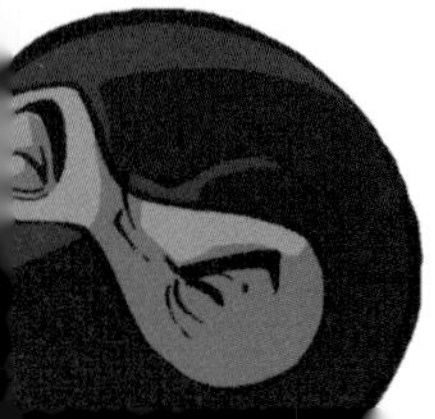

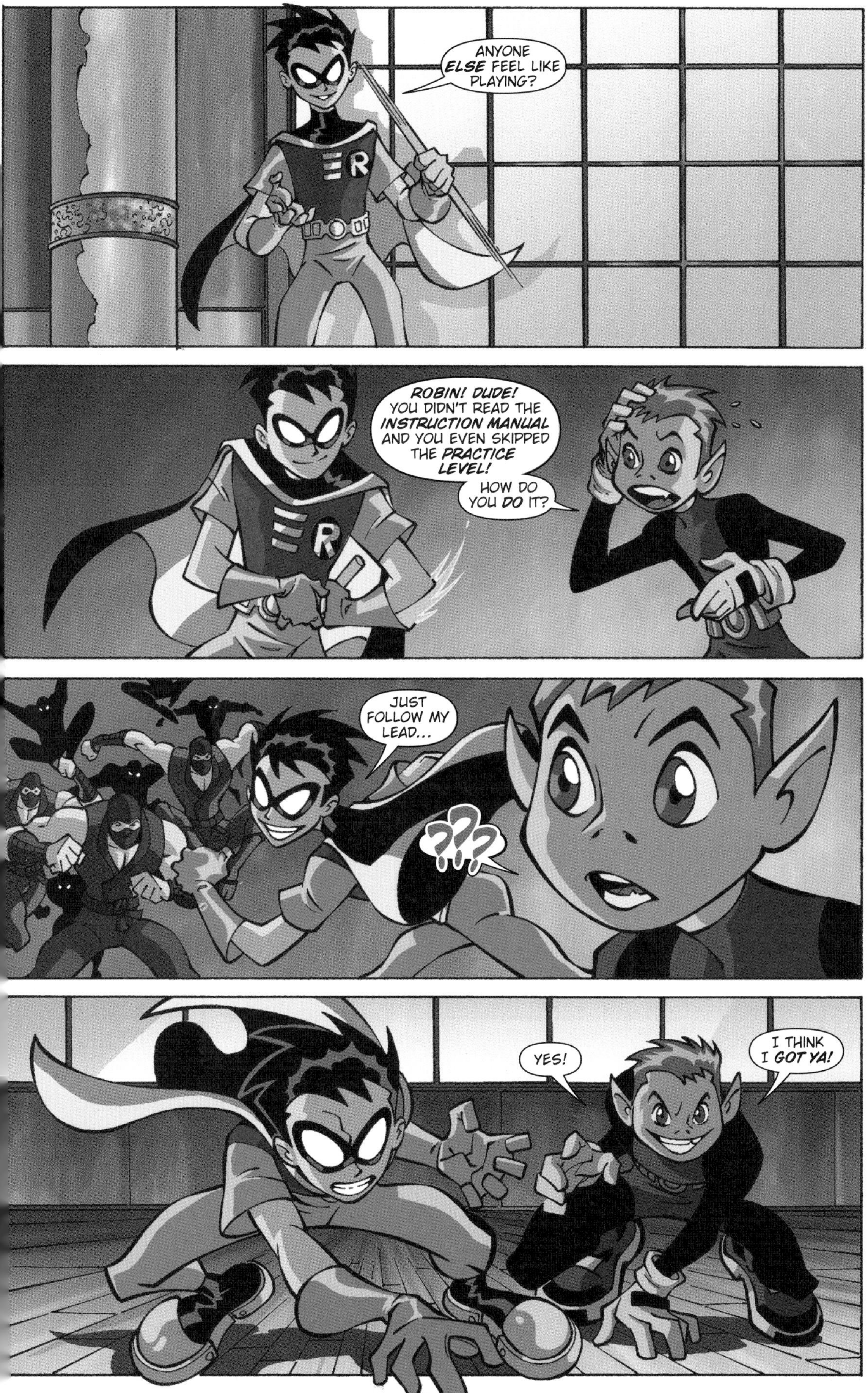
ANYONE ELSE FEEL LIKE PLAYING?
ROBIN! DUDE! YOU DIDN'T READ THE INSTRUCTION MANUAL AND YOU EVEN SKIPPED THE PRACTICE LEVEL!
HOW DO YOU DO IT?
JUST FOLLOW MY LEAD...
???
YES!
I THINK I GOT YA!

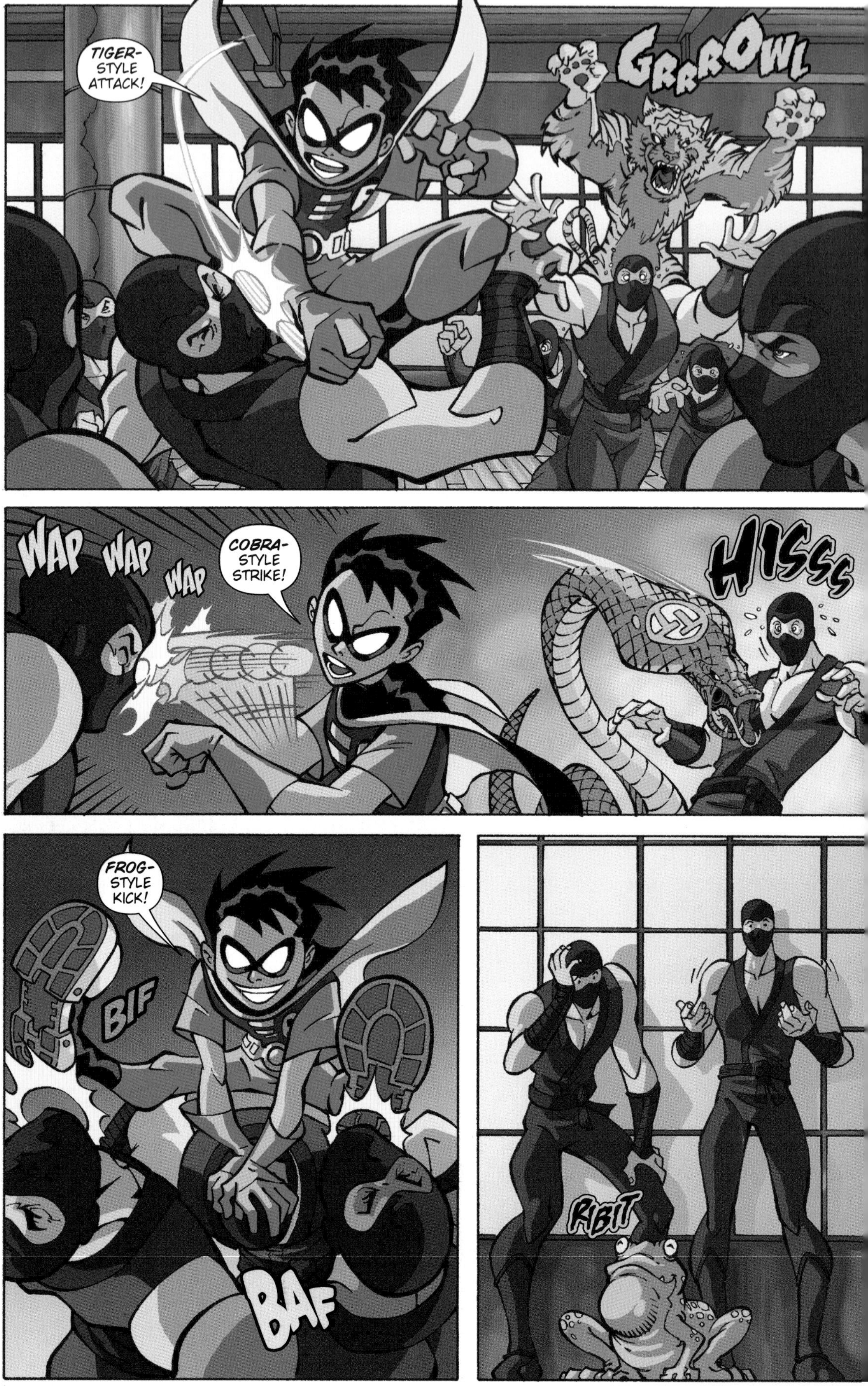
TIGER-STYLE ATTACK!
GRRROWL
WAP WAP WAP
COBRA-STYLE STRIKE!
HISSS
FROG-STYLE KICK!
BIF
BAF
RIBIT

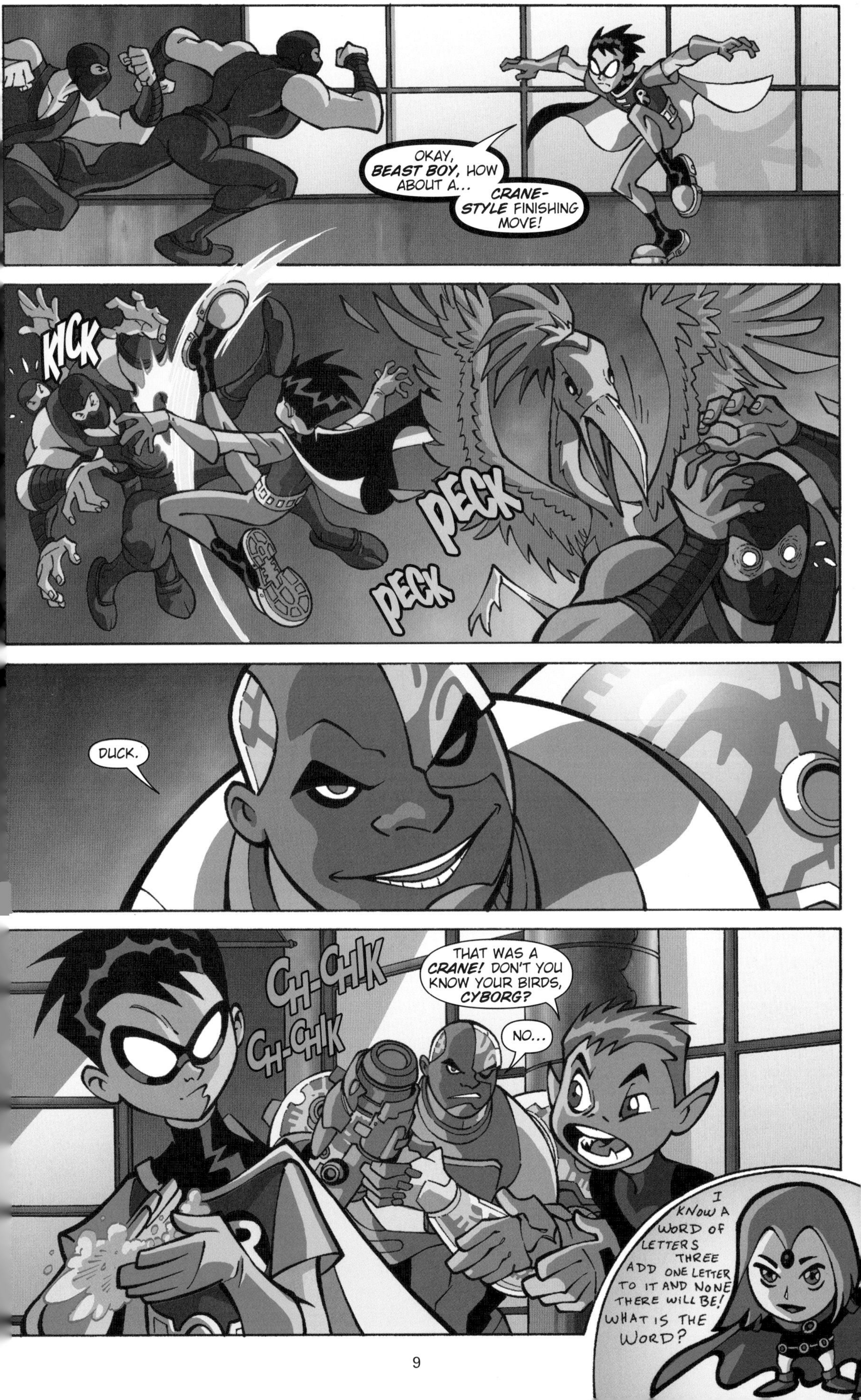
OKAY, BEAST BOY, HOW ABOUT A...
CRANE-STYLE FINISHING MOVE!
KICK
PECK
PECK
DUCK.
CH-CHIK
CH-CHIK
THAT WAS A CRANE! DON'T YOU KNOW YOUR BIRDS, CYBORG?
NO...
I KNOW A WORD OF LETTERS THREE ADD ONE LETTER TO IT AND NONE THERE WILL BE! WHAT IS THE WORD?

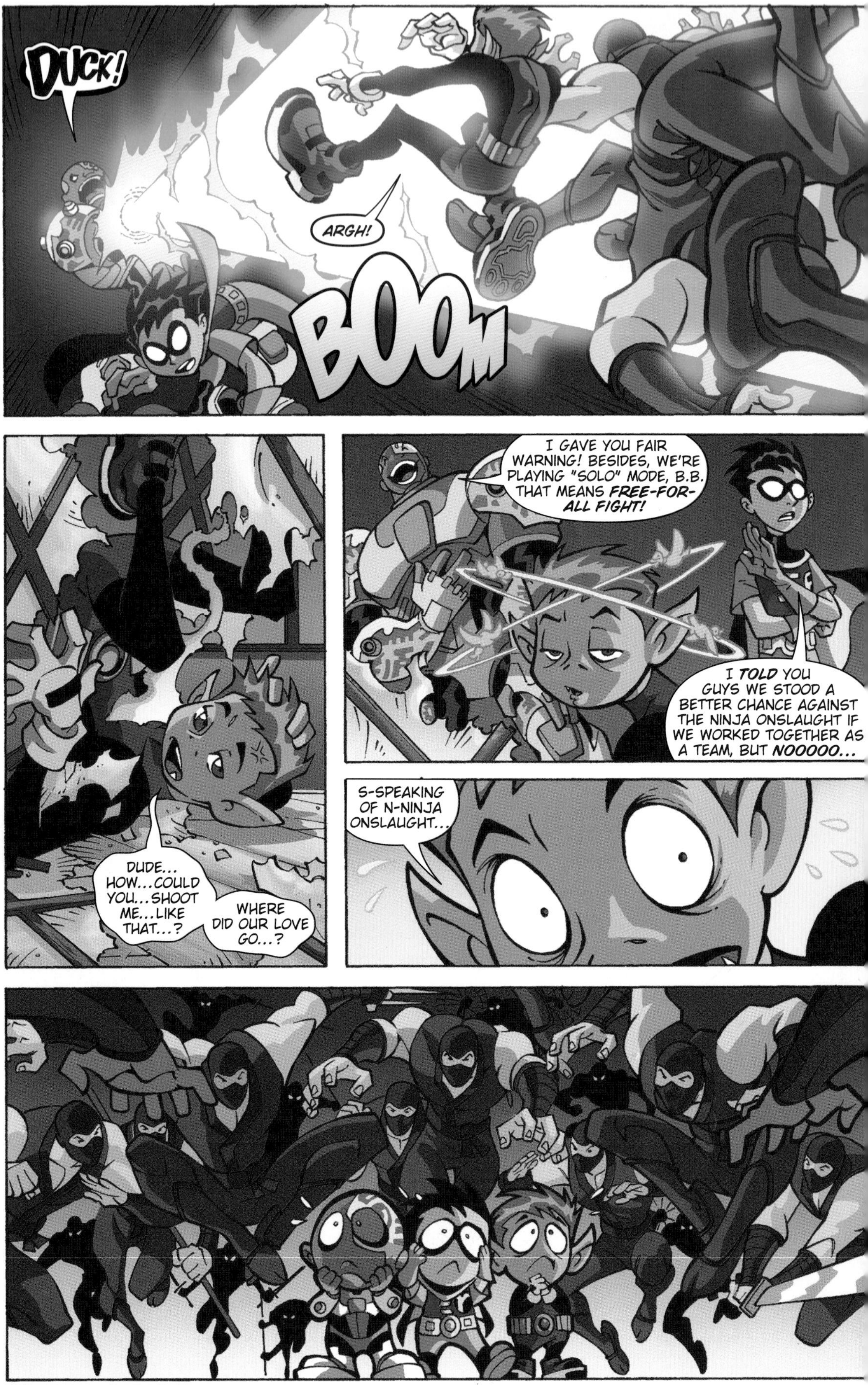
DUCK!
ARGH!
BOOM
DUDE... HOW...COULD YOU...SHOOT ME...LIKE THAT...?
WHERE DID OUR LOVE GO...?
I GAVE YOU FAIR WARNING! BESIDES, WE'RE PLAYING "SOLO" MODE, B.B. THAT MEANS FREE-FOR-ALL FIGHT!
I TOLD YOU GUYS WE STOOD A BETTER CHANCE AGAINST THE NINJA ONSLAUGHT IF WE WORKED TOGETHER AS A TEAM, BUT NOOOOO...
S-SPEAKING OF N-NINJA ONSLAUGHT...

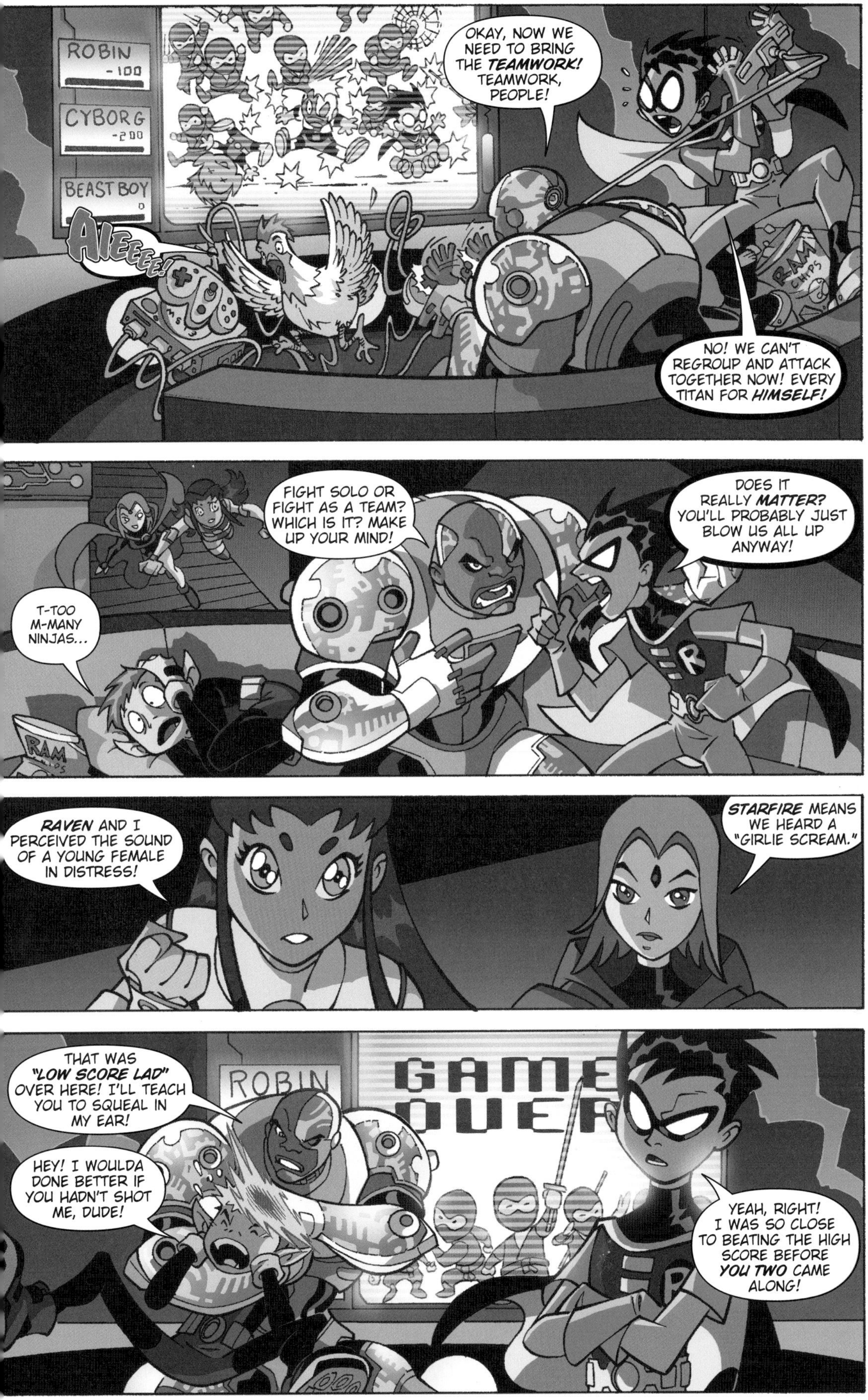
ROBIN -100
CYBORG -200
BEAST BOY 0
AIEEEEE!
OKAY, NOW WE NEED TO BRING THE TEAMWORK! TEAMWORK, PEOPLE!
NO! WE CAN'T REGROUP AND ATTACK TOGETHER NOW! EVERY TITAN FOR HIMSELF!
FIGHT SOLO OR FIGHT AS A TEAM? WHICH IS IT? MAKE UP YOUR MIND!
DOES IT REALLY MATTER? YOU'LL PROBABLY JUST BLOW US ALL UP ANYWAY!
T-TOO M-MANY NINJAS...
RAVEN AND I PERCEIVED THE SOUND OF A YOUNG FEMALE IN DISTRESS!
STARFIRE MEANS WE HEARD A "GIRLIE SCREAM."
ROBIN
GAME OVER
THAT WAS "LOW SCORE LAD" OVER HERE! I'LL TEACH YOU TO SQUEAL IN MY EAR!
HEY! I WOULDA DONE BETTER IF YOU HADN'T SHOT ME, DUDE!
YEAH, RIGHT! I WAS SO CLOSE TO BEATING THE HIGH SCORE BEFORE YOU TWO CAME ALONG!

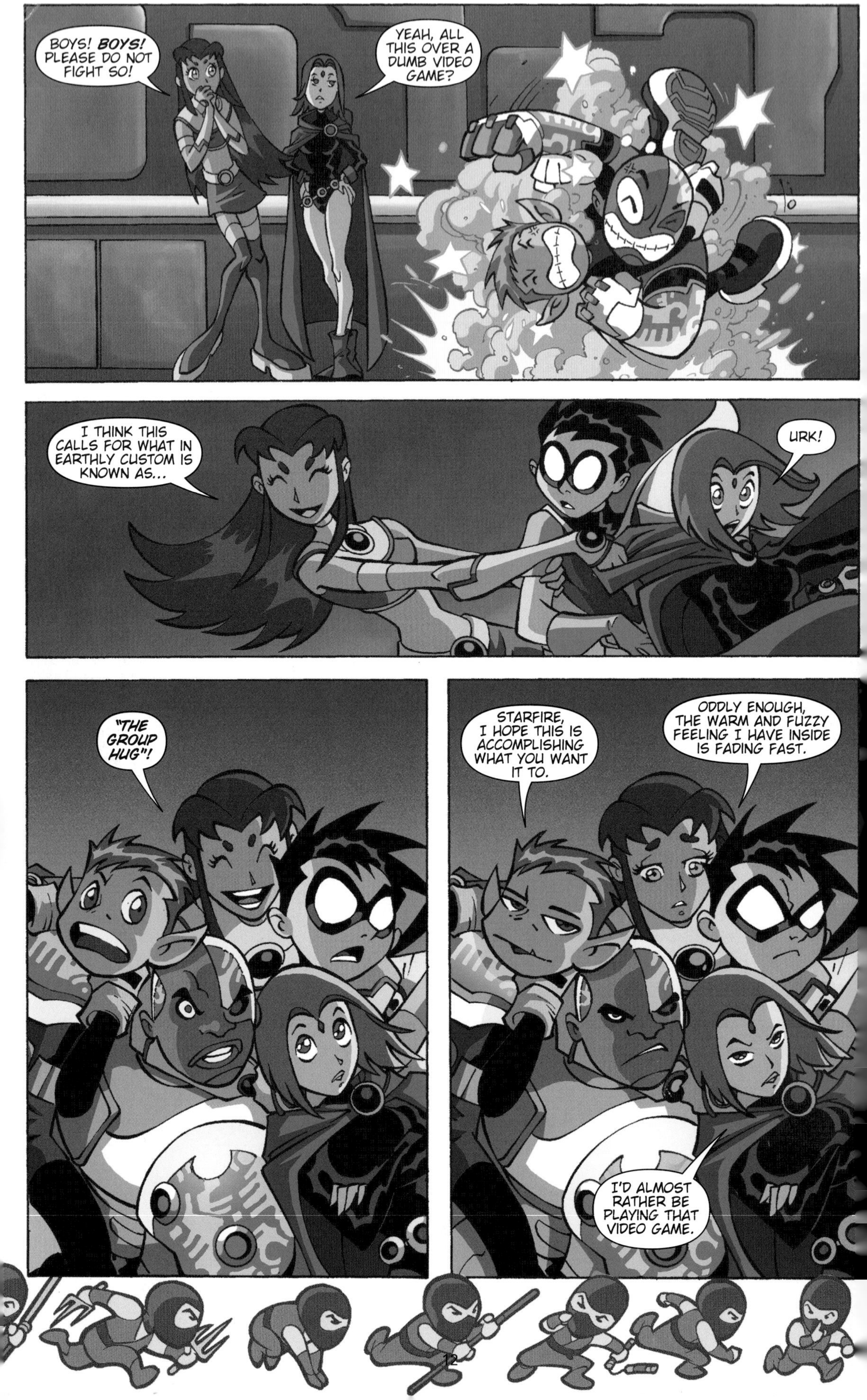

BOYS! BOYS! PLEASE DO NOT FIGHT SO!
YEAH, ALL THIS OVER A DUMB VIDEO GAME?
I THINK THIS CALLS FOR WHAT IN EARTHLY CUSTOM IS KNOWN AS...
URK!
"THE GROUP HUG"!
STARFIRE, I HOPE THIS IS ACCOMPLISHING WHAT YOU WANT IT TO.
ODDLY ENOUGH, THE WARM AND FUZZY FEELING I HAVE INSIDE IS FADING FAST.
I'D ALMOST RATHER BE PLAYING THAT VIDEO GAME.

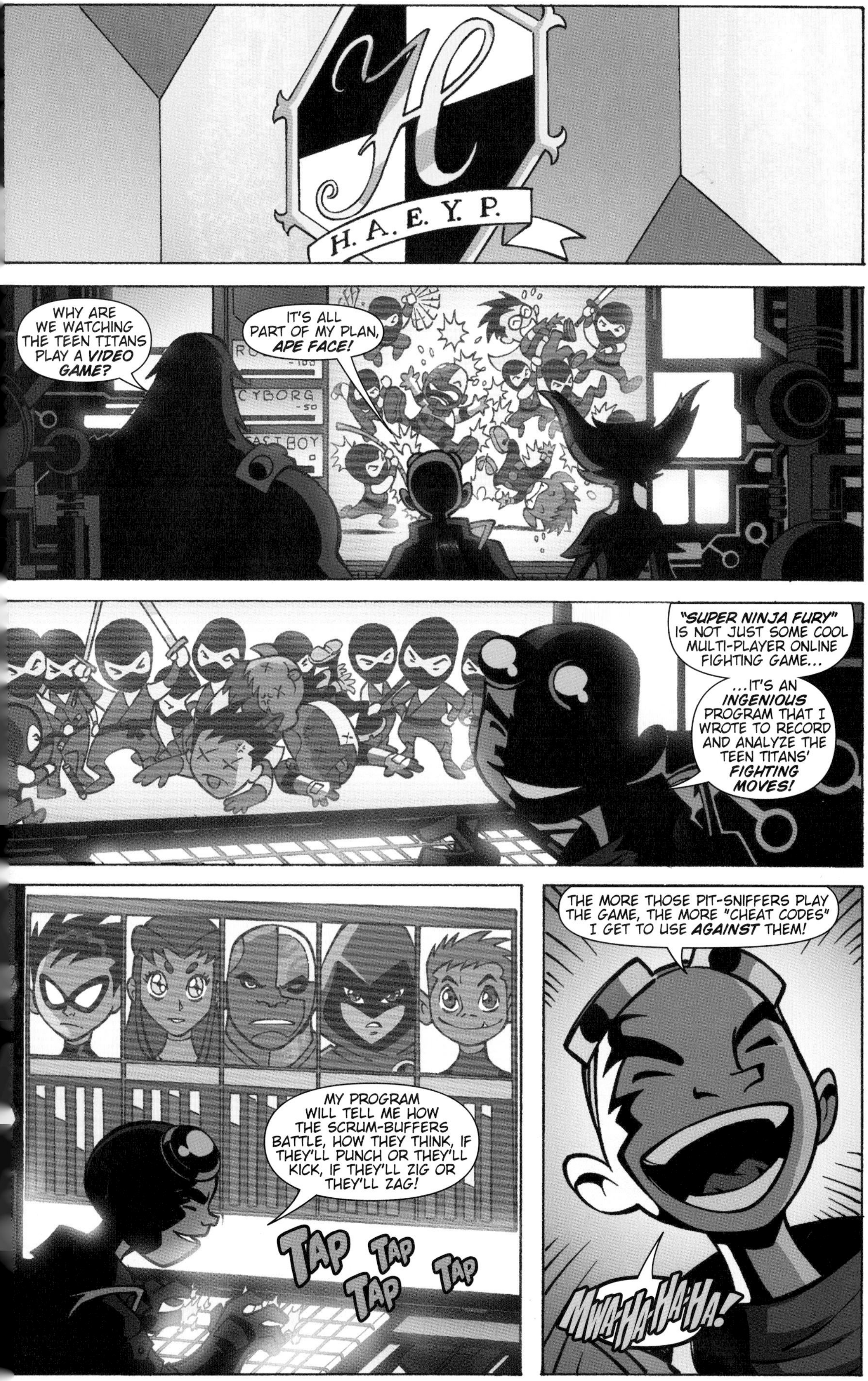
H.A.E.Y.P.
WHY ARE WE WATCHING THE TEEN TITANS PLAY A *VIDEO GAME?*
IT'S ALL PART OF MY PLAN, *APE FACE!*
CYBORG
-50
"SUPER NINJA FURY" IS NOT JUST SOME COOL MULTI-PLAYER ONLINE FIGHTING GAME...
...IT'S AN *INGENIOUS* PROGRAM THAT I WROTE TO RECORD AND ANALYZE THE TEEN TITANS' *FIGHTING MOVES!*
MY PROGRAM WILL TELL ME HOW THE SCRUM-BUFFERS BATTLE, HOW THEY THINK, IF THEY'LL PUNCH OR THEY'LL KICK, IF THEY'LL ZIG OR THEY'LL ZAG!
TAP TAP TAP TAP
THE MORE THOSE PIT-SNIFFERS PLAY THE GAME, THE MORE "CHEAT CODES" I GET TO USE *AGAINST* THEM!
MWA-HA-HA-HA!

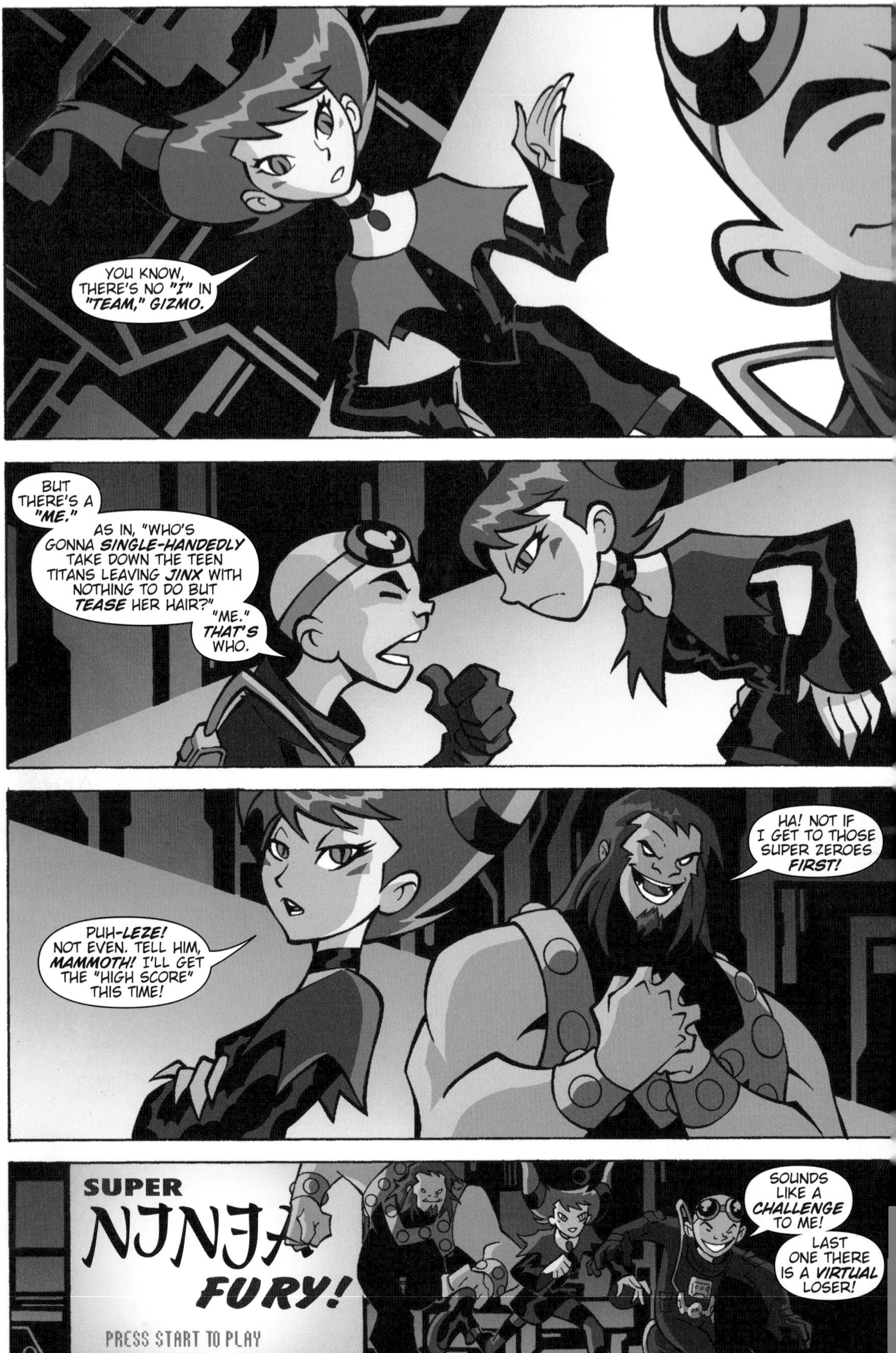
YOU KNOW, THERE'S NO "I" IN "TEAM," GIZMO.
BUT THERE'S A "ME."
AS IN, "WHO'S GONNA SINGLE-HANDEDLY TAKE DOWN THE TEEN TITANS LEAVING JINX WITH NOTHING TO DO BUT TEASE HER HAIR?"
"ME." THAT'S WHO.
HA! NOT IF I GET TO THOSE SUPER ZEROES FIRST!
PUH-LEZE! NOT EVEN. TELL HIM, MAMMOTH! I'LL GET THE "HIGH SCORE" THIS TIME!
SUPER NINJA FURY!
PRESS START TO PLAY
SOUNDS LIKE A CHALLENGE TO ME!
LAST ONE THERE IS A VIRTUAL LOSER!

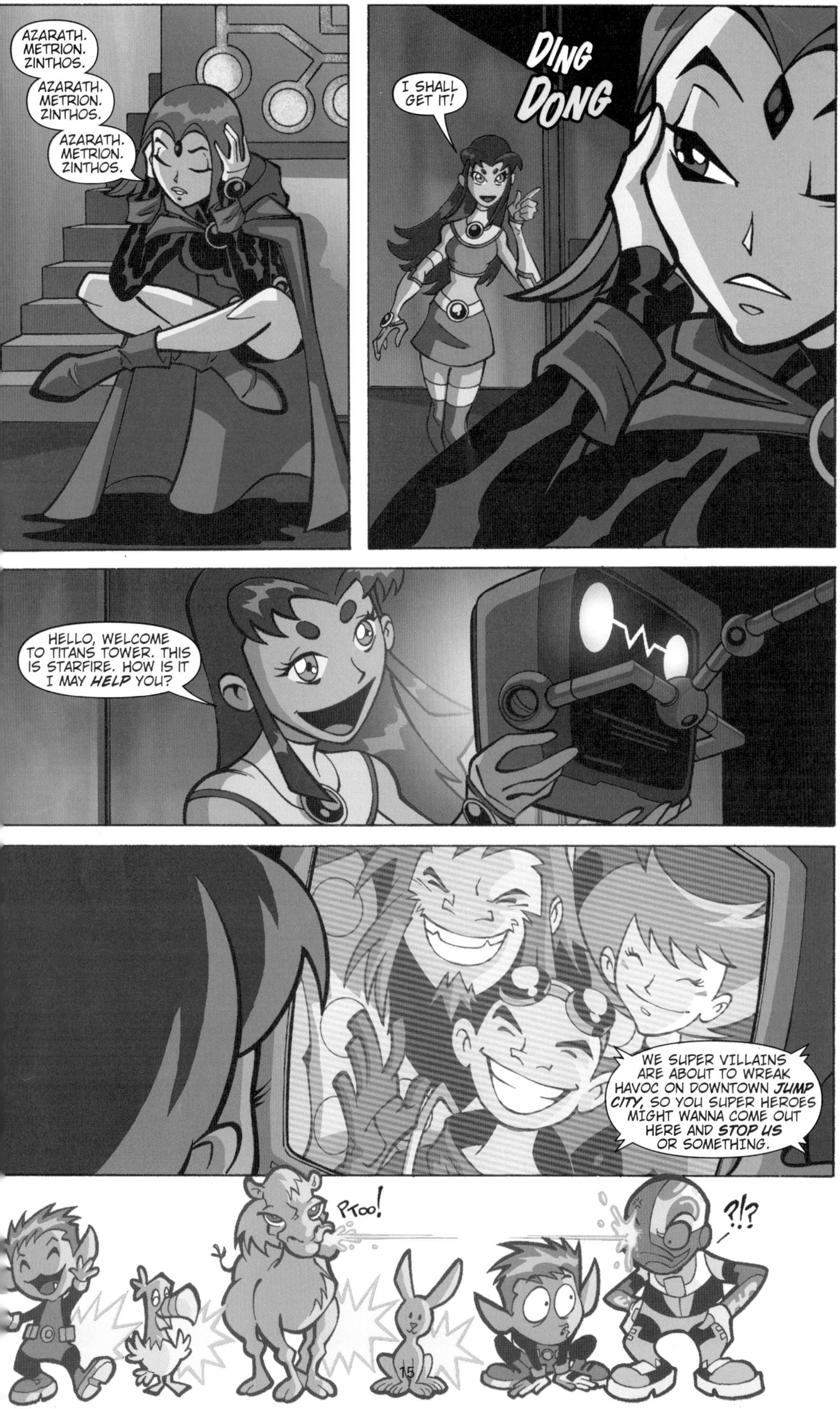
AZARATH. METRION. ZINTHOS.
AZARATH. METRION. ZINTHOS.
AZARATH. METRION. ZINTHOS.
I SHALL GET IT!
DING DONG
HELLO, WELCOME TO TITANS TOWER. THIS IS STARFIRE. HOW IS IT I MAY **HELP** YOU?
WE SUPER VILLAINS ARE ABOUT TO WREAK HAVOC ON DOWNTOWN ***JUMP CITY***, SO YOU SUPER HEROES MIGHT WANNA COME OUT HERE AND ***STOP US*** OR SOMETHING.
PTOO!
?!?

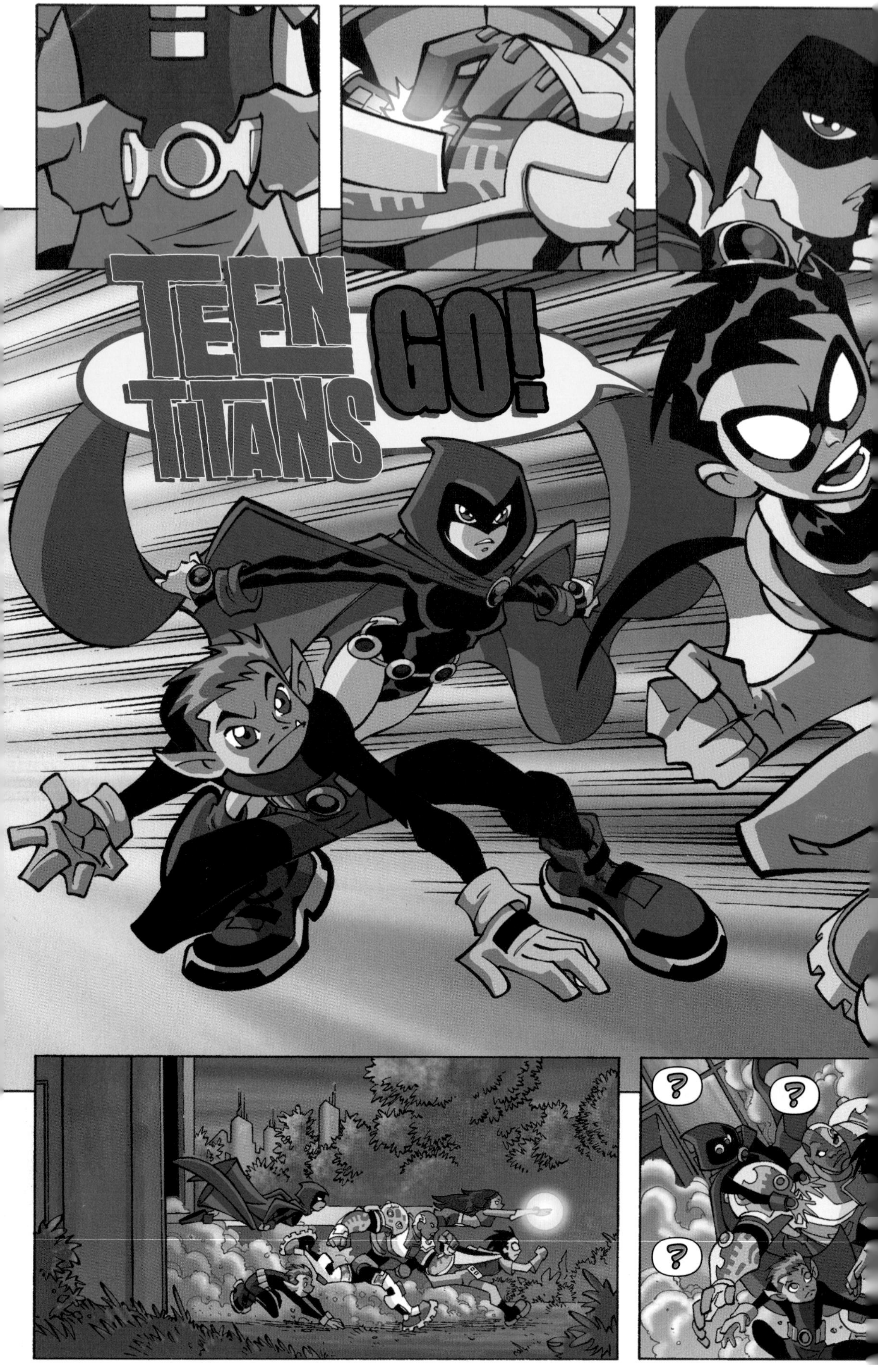
TEEN TITANS GO!
?
?
?

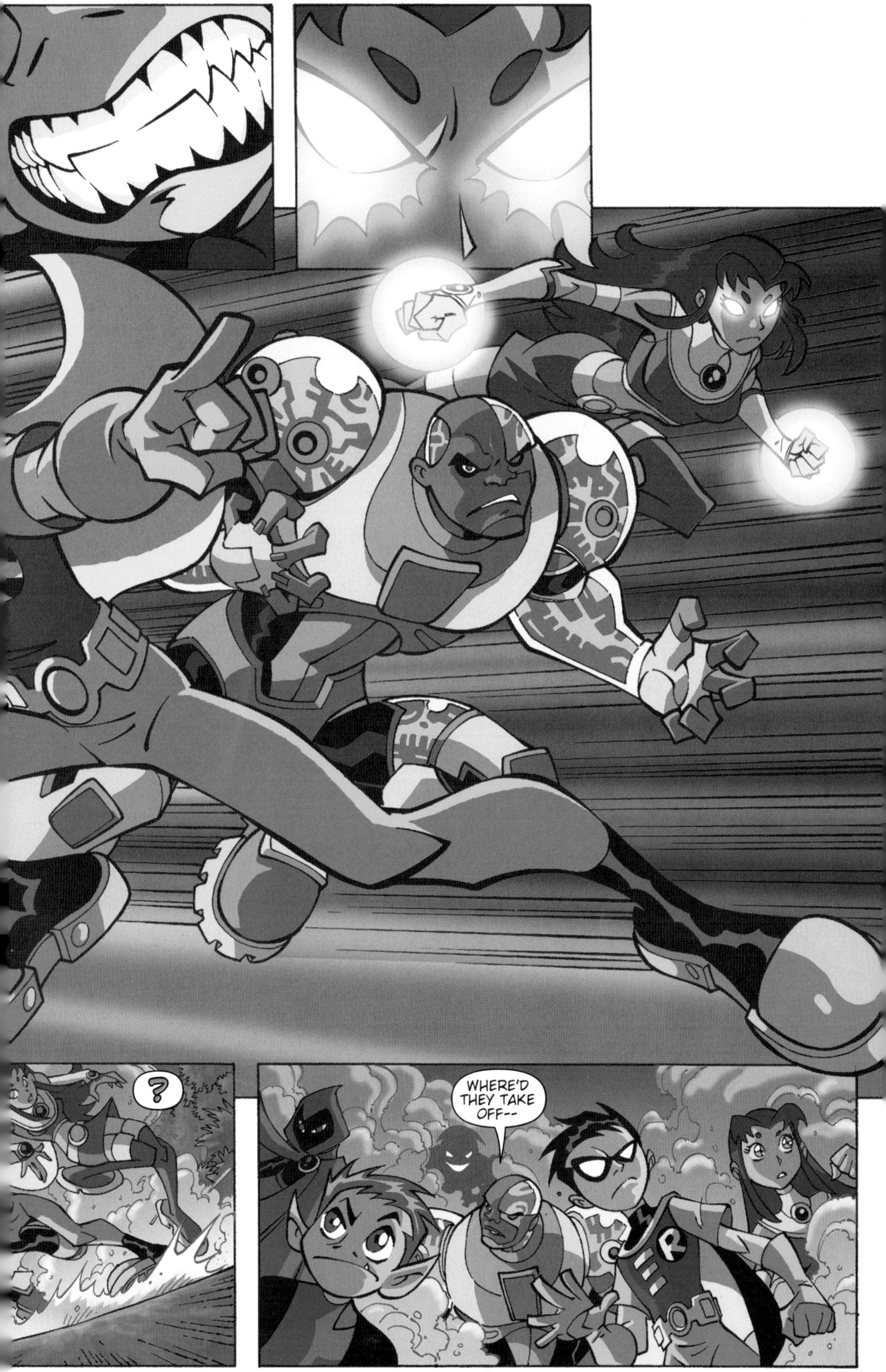
?
WHERE'D THEY TAKE OFF--

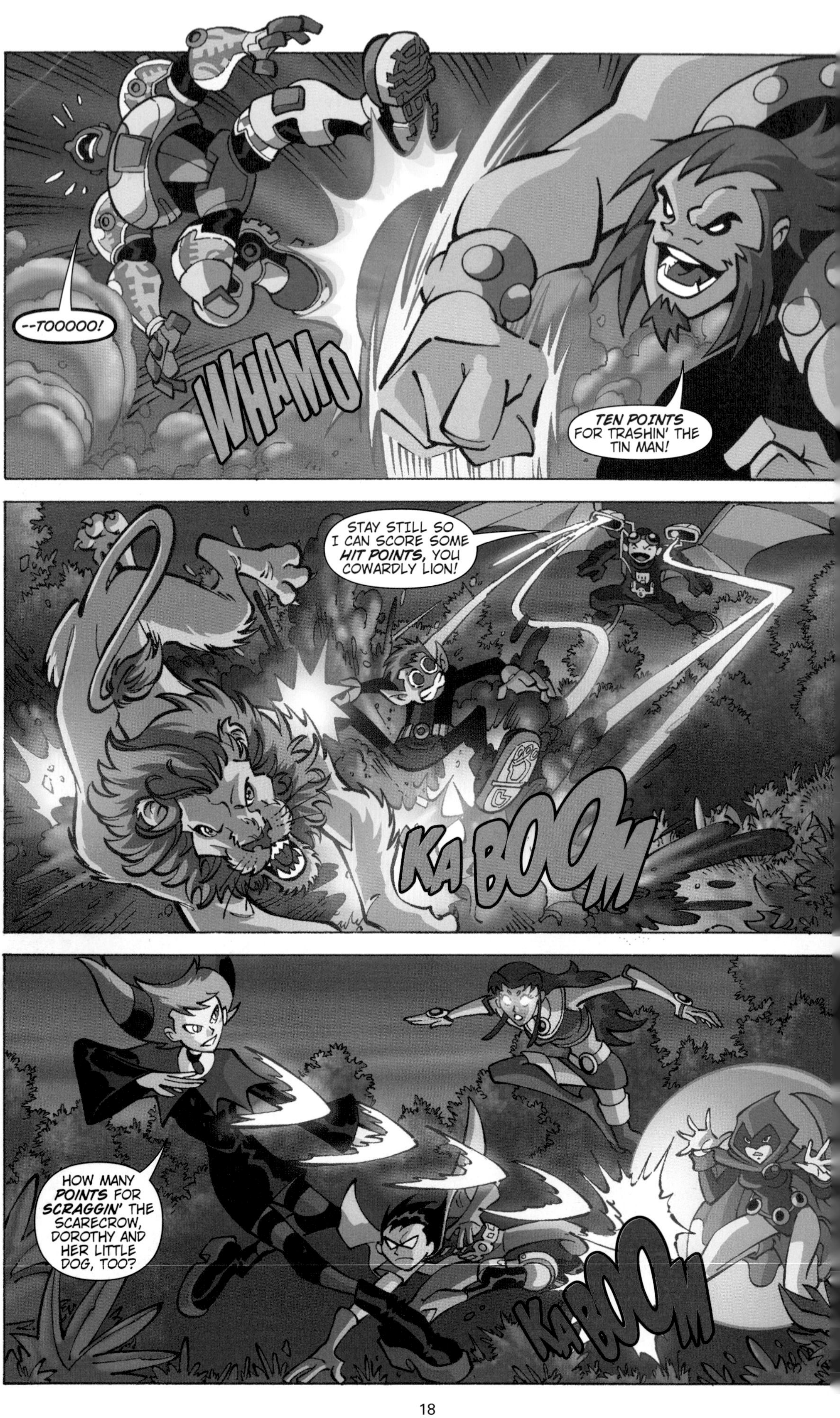

--TOOOOO!
WHAMO
TEN POINTS FOR TRASHIN' THE TIN MAN!
STAY STILL SO I CAN SCORE SOME HIT POINTS, YOU COWARDLY LION!
KA BOOM
HOW MANY POINTS FOR SCRAGGIN' THE SCARECROW, DOROTHY AND HER LITTLE DOG, TOO?
KABOOM

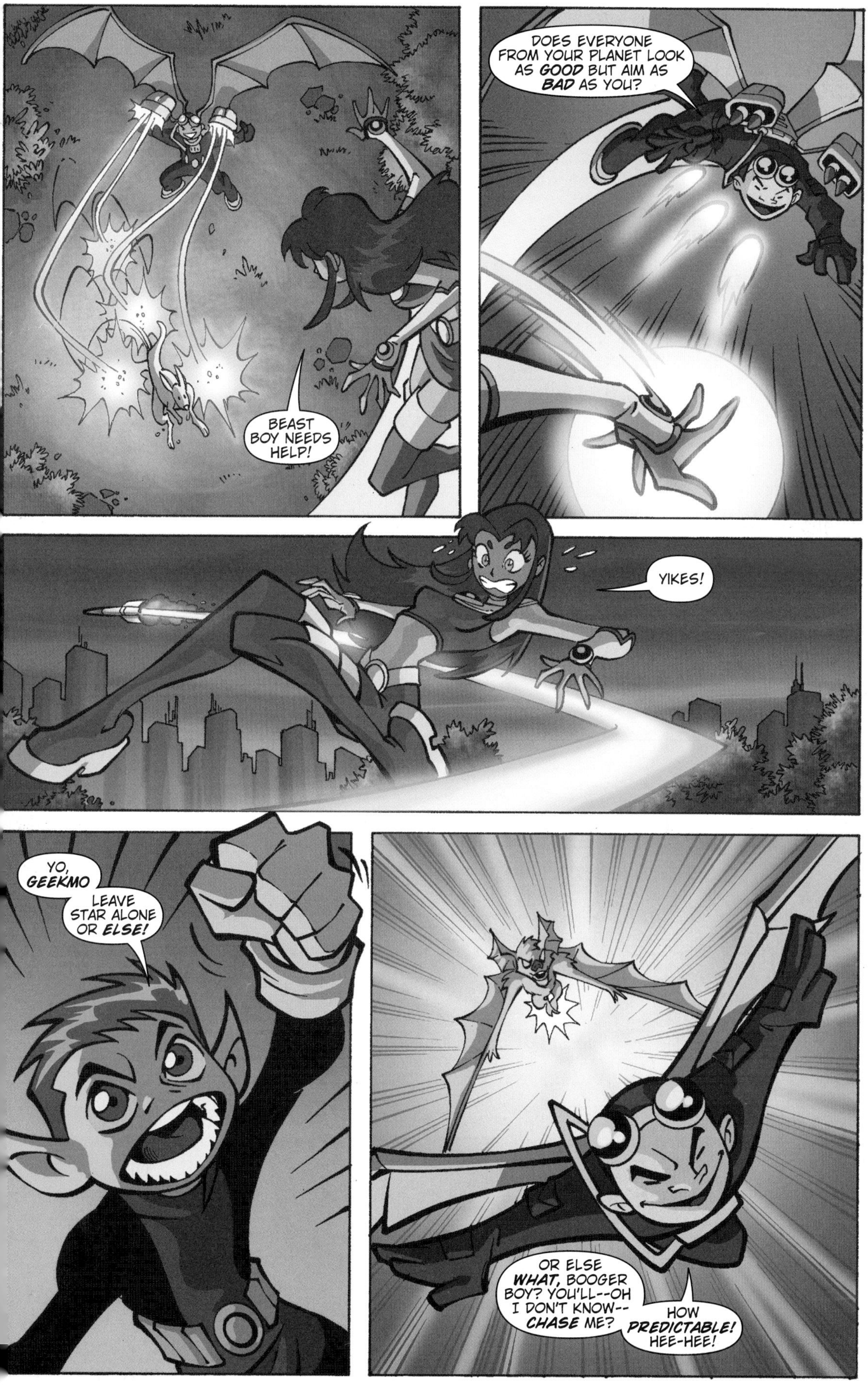
BEAST BOY NEEDS HELP!
DOES EVERYONE FROM YOUR PLANET LOOK AS **GOOD** BUT AIM AS **BAD** AS YOU?
YIKES!
YO, **GEEKMO**
LEAVE STAR ALONE OR **ELSE!**
OR ELSE **WHAT,** BOOGER BOY? YOU'LL--OH I DON'T KNOW-- **CHASE** ME?
HOW **PREDICTABLE!** HEE-HEE!

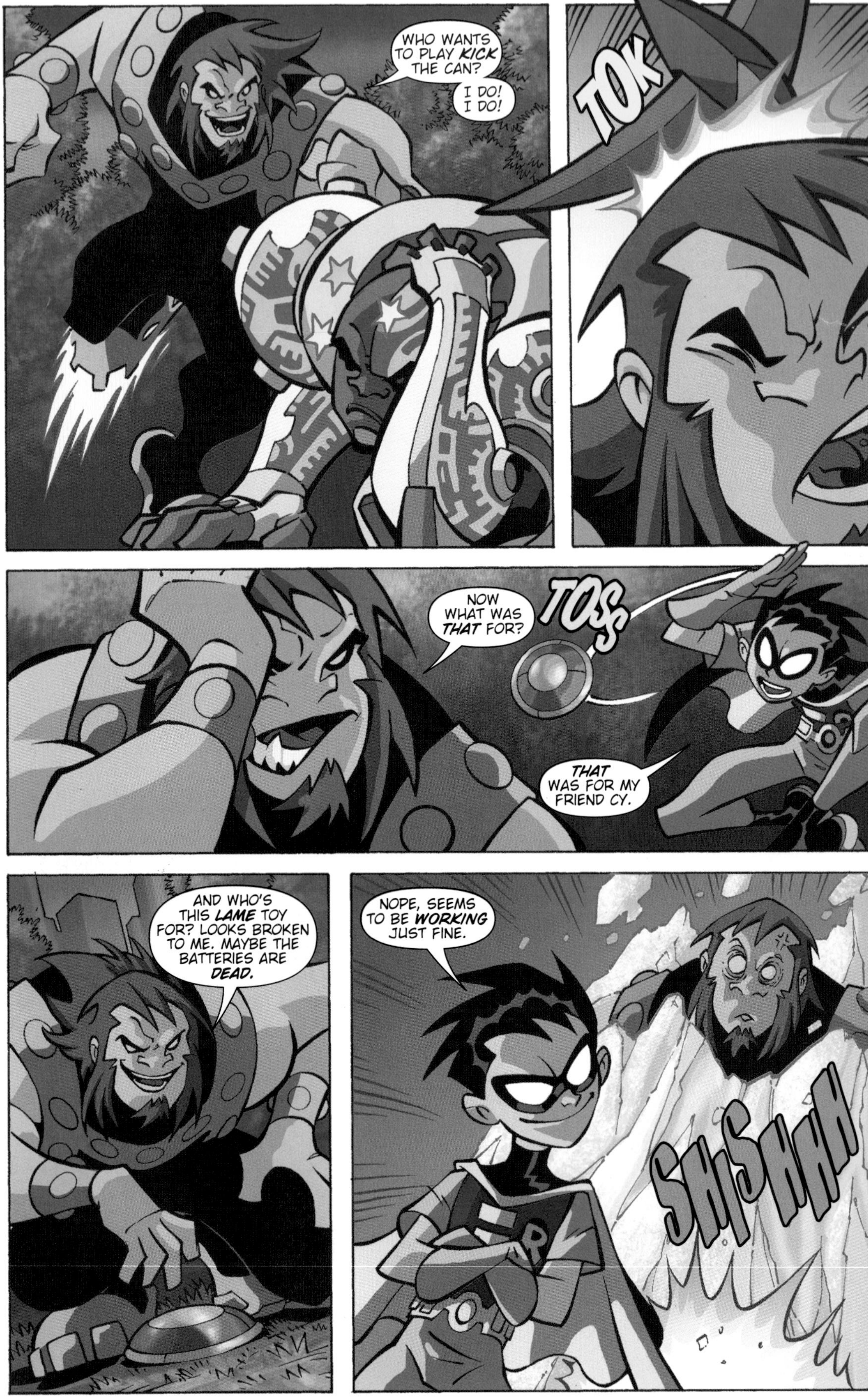

WHO WANTS TO PLAY KICK THE CAN?
I DO! I DO!
TOK
NOW WHAT WAS THAT FOR?
TOSS
THAT WAS FOR MY FRIEND CY.
AND WHO'S THIS LAME TOY FOR? LOOKS BROKEN TO ME. MAYBE THE BATTERIES ARE DEAD.
NOPE, SEEMS TO BE WORKING JUST FINE.
SHHSHHH

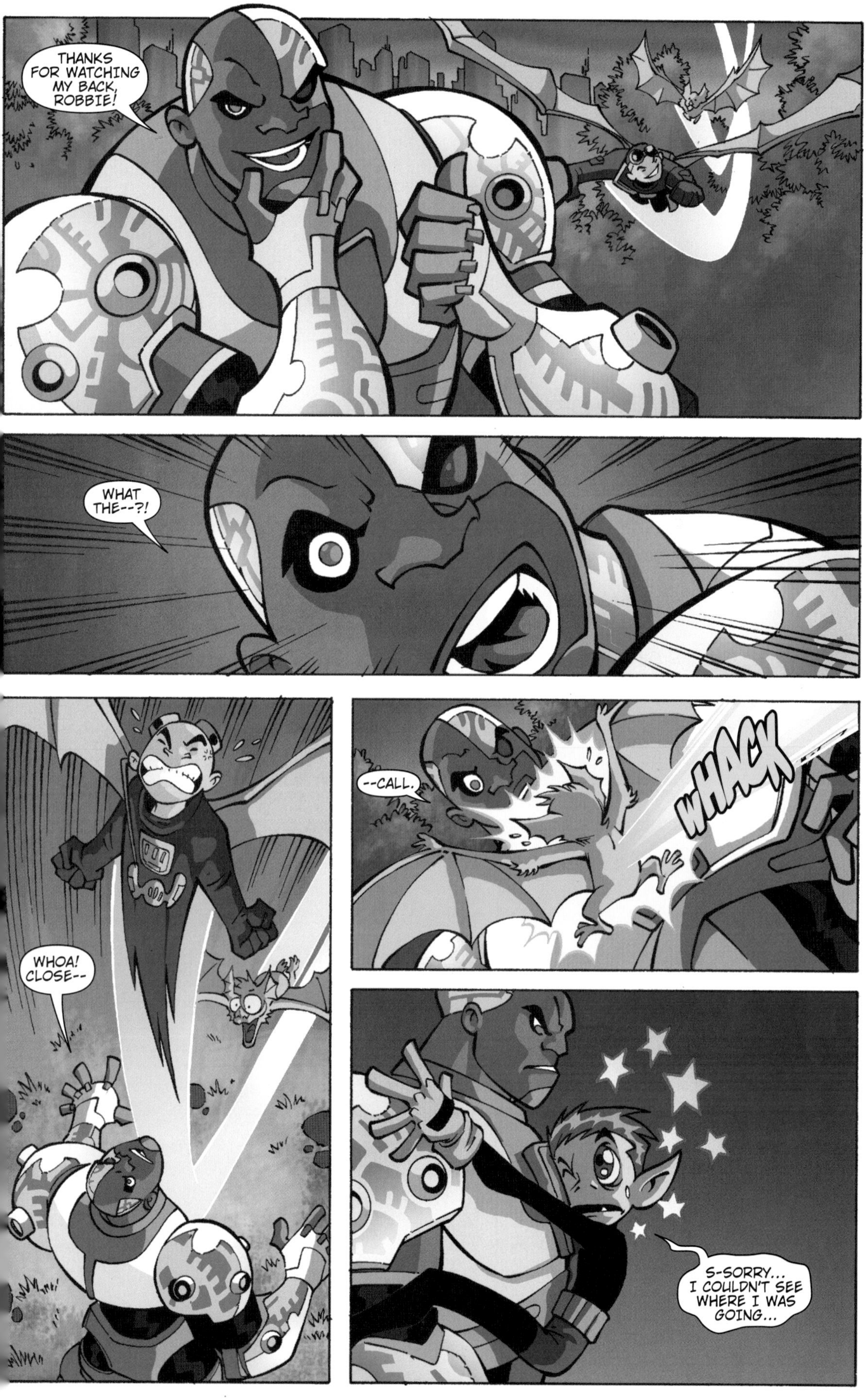
THANKS FOR WATCHING MY BACK, ROBBIE!
WHAT THE--?!
WHOA! CLOSE--
--CALL.
WHACK
S-SORRY... I COULDN'T SEE WHERE I WAS GOING...

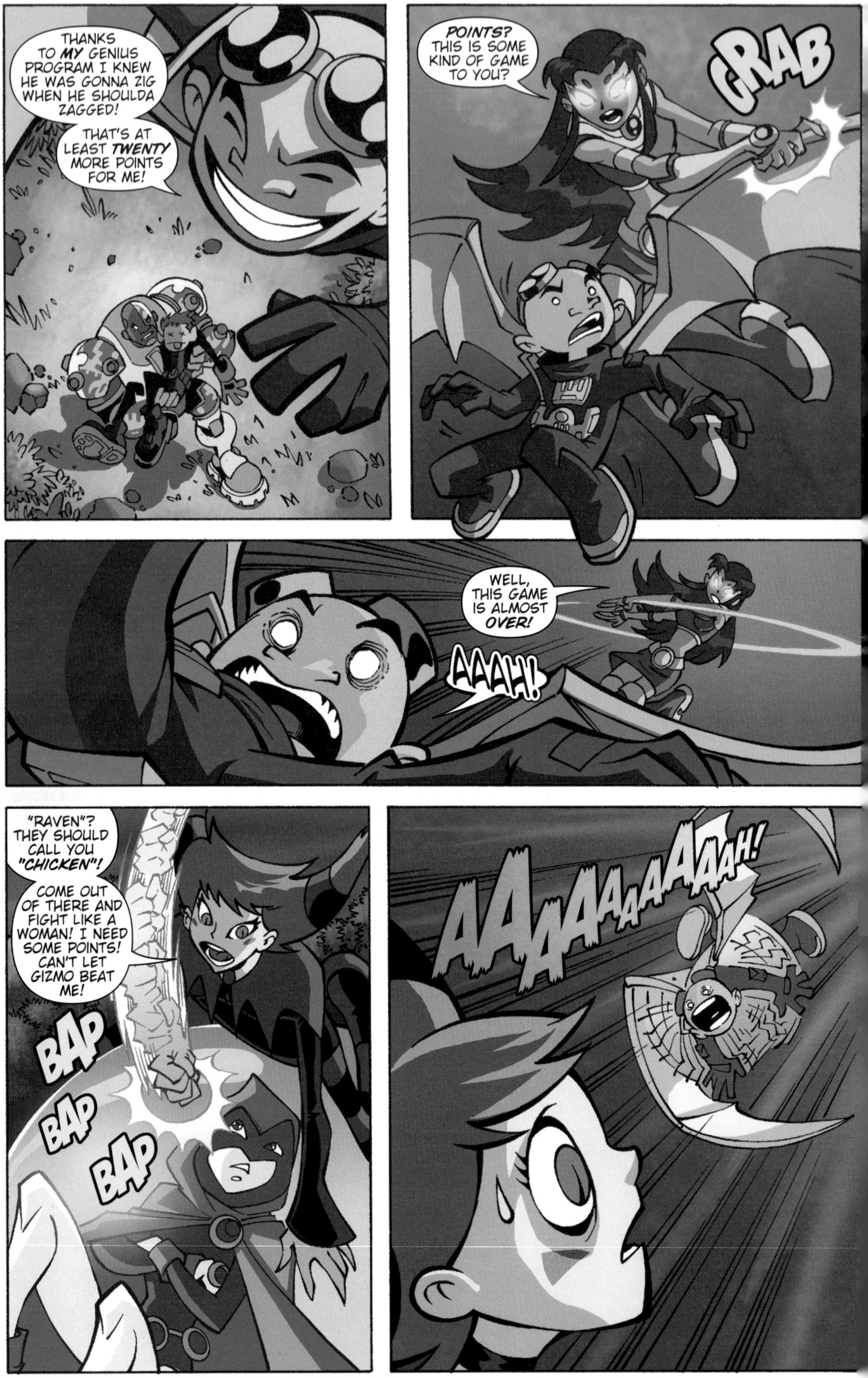
THANKS TO MY GENIUS PROGRAM I KNEW HE WAS GONNA ZIG WHEN HE SHOULDA ZAGGED!
THAT'S AT LEAST TWENTY MORE POINTS FOR ME!
POINTS? THIS IS SOME KIND OF GAME TO YOU?
GRAB
WELL, THIS GAME IS ALMOST OVER!
AAAH!
"RAVEN"? THEY SHOULD CALL YOU "CHICKEN"!
COME OUT OF THERE AND FIGHT LIKE A WOMAN! I NEED SOME POINTS! CAN'T LET GIZMO BEAT ME!
BAP
BAP
BAP
AAAAAAAAAAAH!

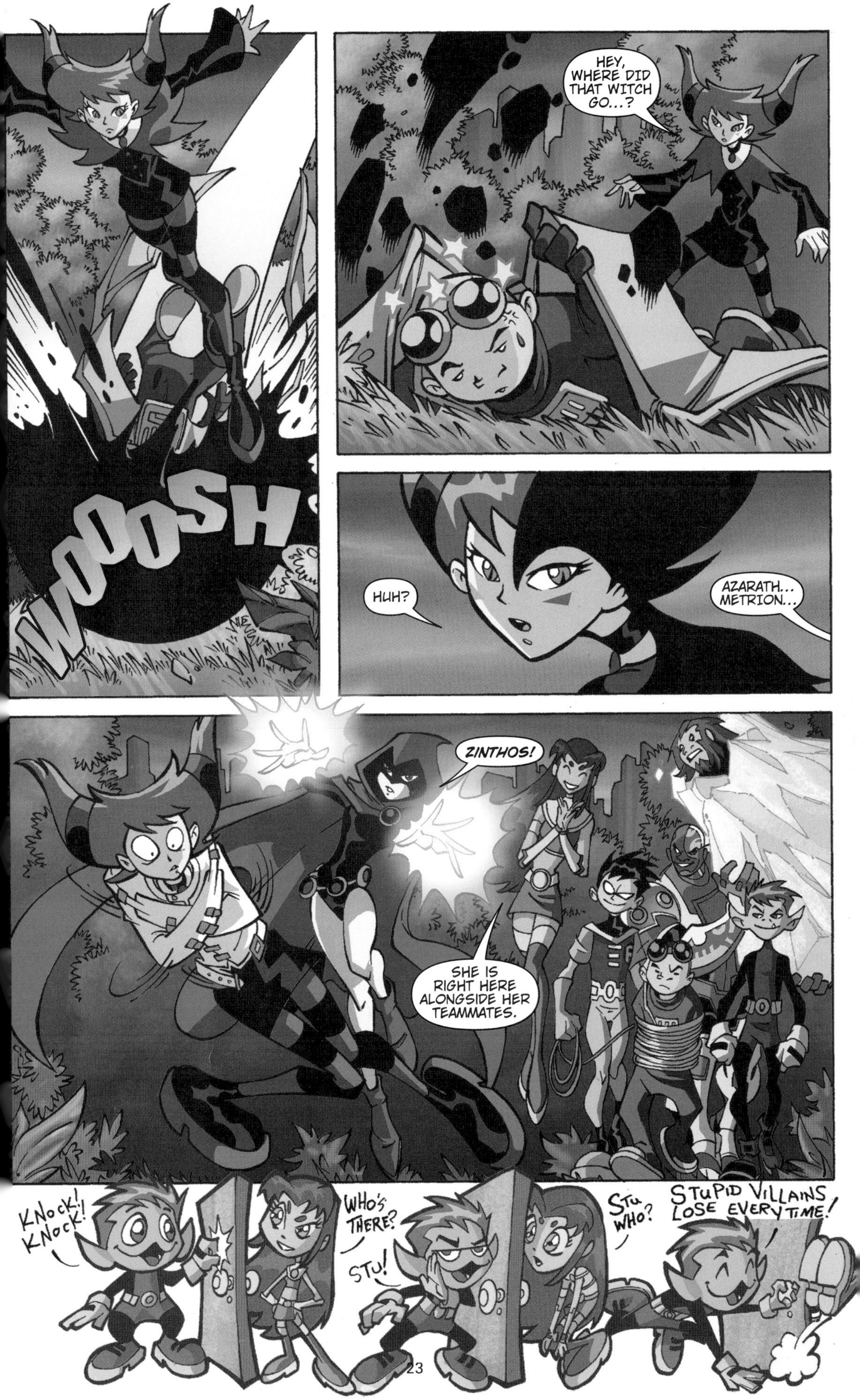
WOOOSH
HEY, WHERE DID THAT WITCH GO...?
HUH?
AZARATH... METRION...
ZINTHOS!
SHE IS RIGHT HERE ALONGSIDE HER TEAMMATES.
KNOCK! KNOCK!
WHO'S THERE?
STU!
STU WHO?
STUPID VILLAINS LOSE EVERY TIME!

BATTLE SIMULATION OVER
MISSION...

FAILED

AHEM.

MY APOLOGIES, MR. SLADE. THIS DEMONSTRATION OF OUR NEW PLAN TO TAKE DOWN THE TEEN TITANS DIDN'T EXACTLY GO AS, ER, PLANNED.

MAMMOTH	GIZMO	JINX
-26/594	-30/452	-18/70

PERHAPS THERE WAS A SLIGHT GLITCH IN THE PROGRAMMING AND THE TITANS' SIMULATED POWER LEVELS WERE SET A LITTLE TOO HIGH SO--

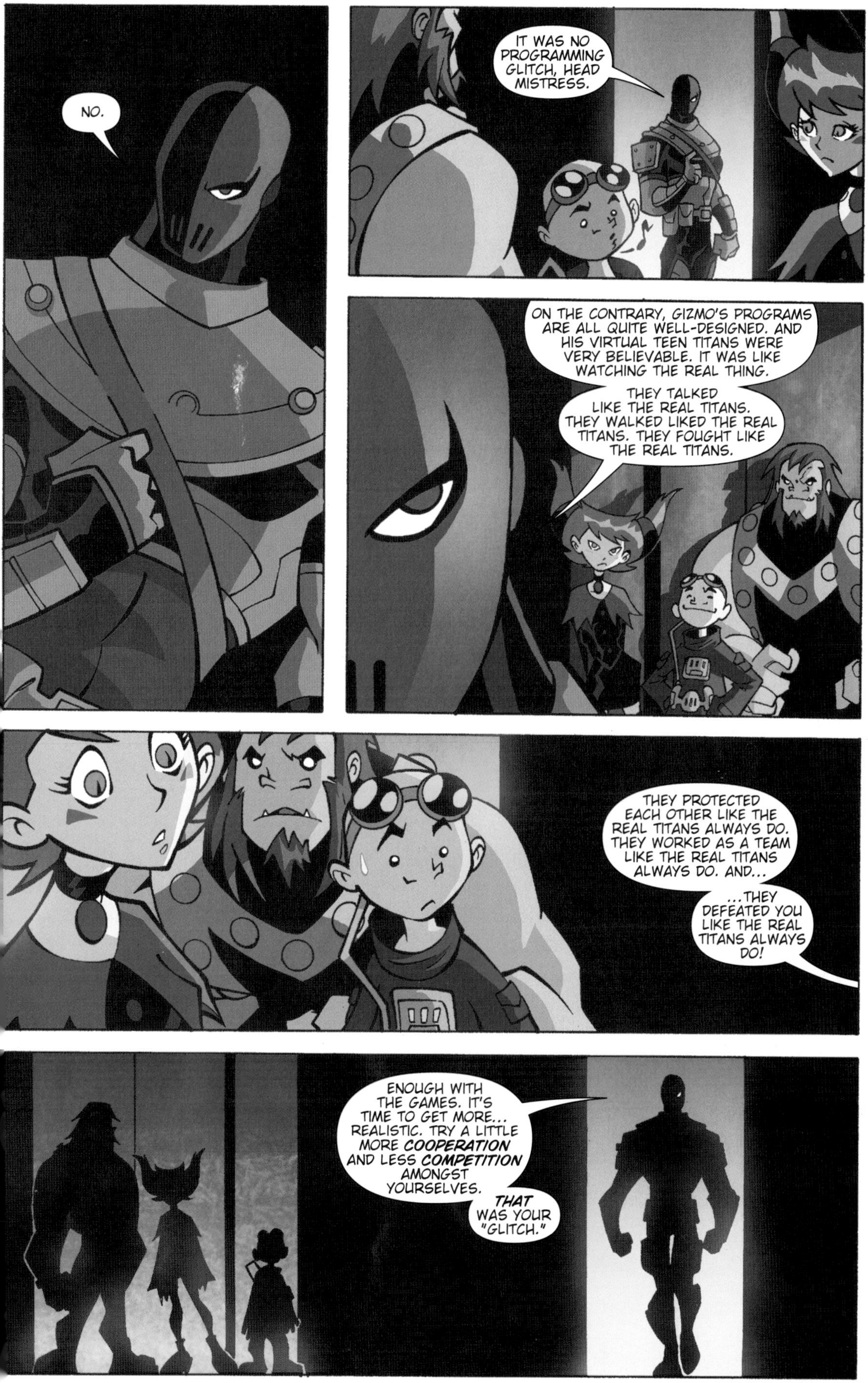
NO.
IT WAS NO PROGRAMMING GLITCH, HEAD MISTRESS.
ON THE CONTRARY, GIZMO'S PROGRAMS ARE ALL QUITE WELL-DESIGNED. AND HIS VIRTUAL TEEN TITANS WERE VERY BELIEVABLE. IT WAS LIKE WATCHING THE REAL THING.
THEY TALKED LIKE THE REAL TITANS. THEY WALKED LIKED THE REAL TITANS. THEY FOUGHT LIKE THE REAL TITANS.
THEY PROTECTED EACH OTHER LIKE THE REAL TITANS ALWAYS DO. THEY WORKED AS A TEAM LIKE THE REAL TITANS ALWAYS DO. AND...
...THEY DEFEATED YOU LIKE THE REAL TITANS ALWAYS DO!
ENOUGH WITH THE GAMES. IT'S TIME TO GET MORE... REALISTIC. TRY A LITTLE MORE COOPERATION AND LESS COMPETITION AMONGST YOURSELVES.
THAT WAS YOUR "GLITCH."

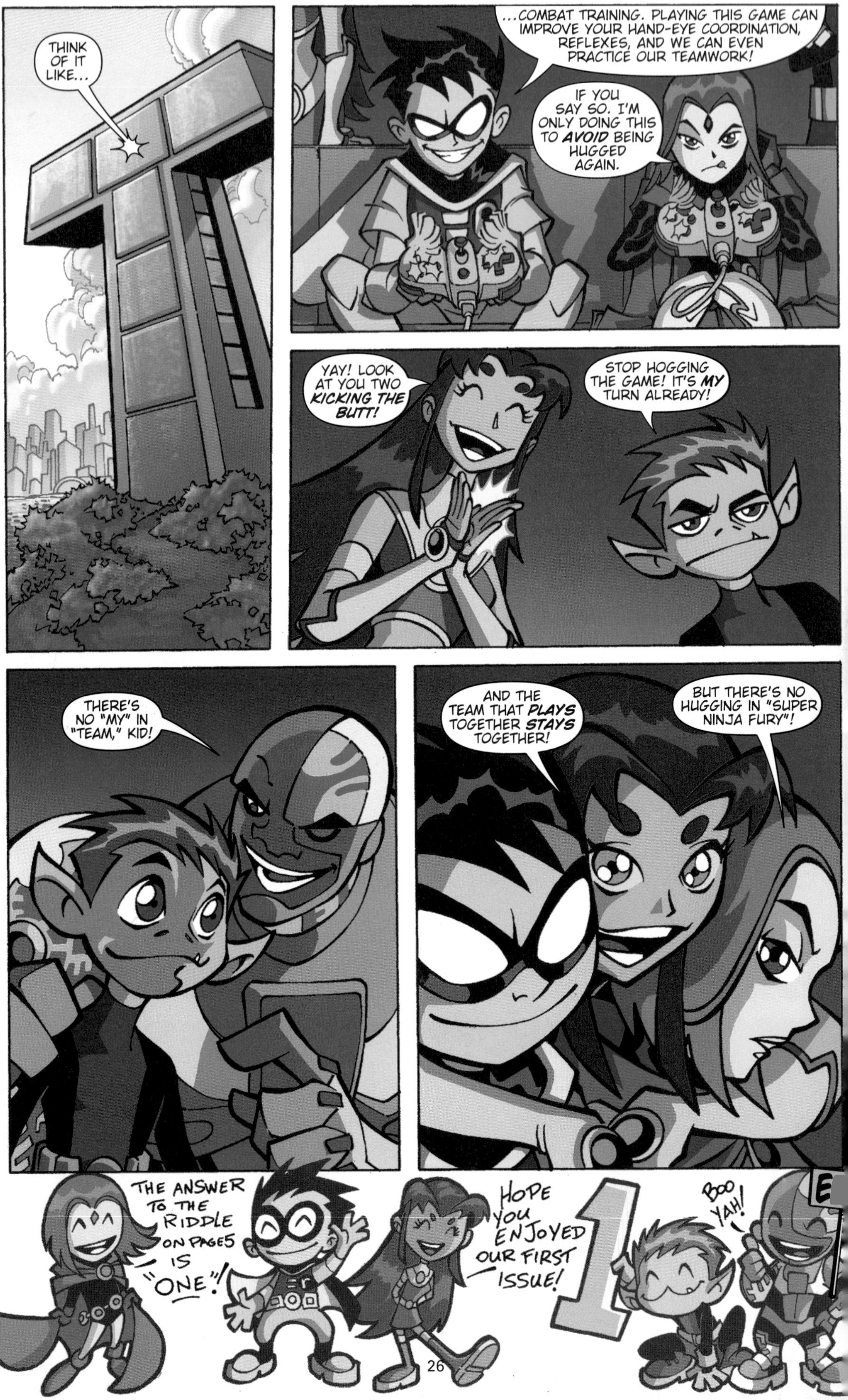

THINK OF IT LIKE...
...COMBAT TRAINING. PLAYING THIS GAME CAN IMPROVE YOUR HAND-EYE COORDINATION, REFLEXES, AND WE CAN EVEN PRACTICE OUR TEAMWORK!
IF YOU SAY SO. I'M ONLY DOING THIS TO AVOID BEING HUGGED AGAIN.
YAY! LOOK AT YOU TWO KICKING THE BUTT!
STOP HOGGING THE GAME! IT'S MY TURN ALREADY!
THERE'S NO "MY" IN "TEAM," KID!
AND THE TEAM THAT PLAYS TOGETHER STAYS TOGETHER!
BUT THERE'S NO HUGGING IN "SUPER NINJA FURY"!
THE ANSWER TO THE RIDDLE ON PAGE 5 IS "ONE"!
HOPE YOU ENJOYED OUR FIRST ISSUE!
BOO YAH!

CREATORS

J. TORRES WRITER

J. Torres won the Shuster Award for Outstanding Writer for his work on Batman: Legends of the Dark Knight, Love As a Foreign Language, and Teen Titans Go! He is also the writer of the Eisner Award nominated Alison Dare and the YALSA listed Days Like This and Lola: A Ghost Story. Other comic book credits include Avatar: The Last Airbender, Batman: The Brave and the Bold, Legion of Super-Heroes in the 31st Century, Ninja Scroll, Wonder Girl, Wonder Woman, and WALL-E: Recharge.

TODD NAUCK ARTIST

Todd Nauck is an American comic book artist and writer. Nauck is most notable for his work on Young Justice, Teen Titans Go!, and his own creation, Wildguard.

GLOSSARY

cowardly (KOW-urd-lee)--lacking courage

distress (diss-TRESS)--a feeling of great discomfort, or in need of help

fury (FYOOR-ee)--violent anger or rage

glitch (GLICH)--any sudden thing that goes wrong or causes a problem, usually with machinery, as in a computer glitch

havoc (HAV-uhk)--great damage and chaos

ingenious (in-JEE-nee-uhss)--clever or inventive

lame (LAYM)--weak or unconvincing

onslaught (ON-slot)--an overwhelming assault or attack

reflexes (REE-fleks-iz)--automatic actions that happen without a person's control or effort

regroup (ree-GROOP)--if a team regroups, it reforms and reorganizes for a second attack

simulated (SIM-yoo-lay-tid)--created a realistic model of something that isn't actually real

wreak (REEK)--to carry out or inflict

VISUAL QUESTIONS & PROMPTS

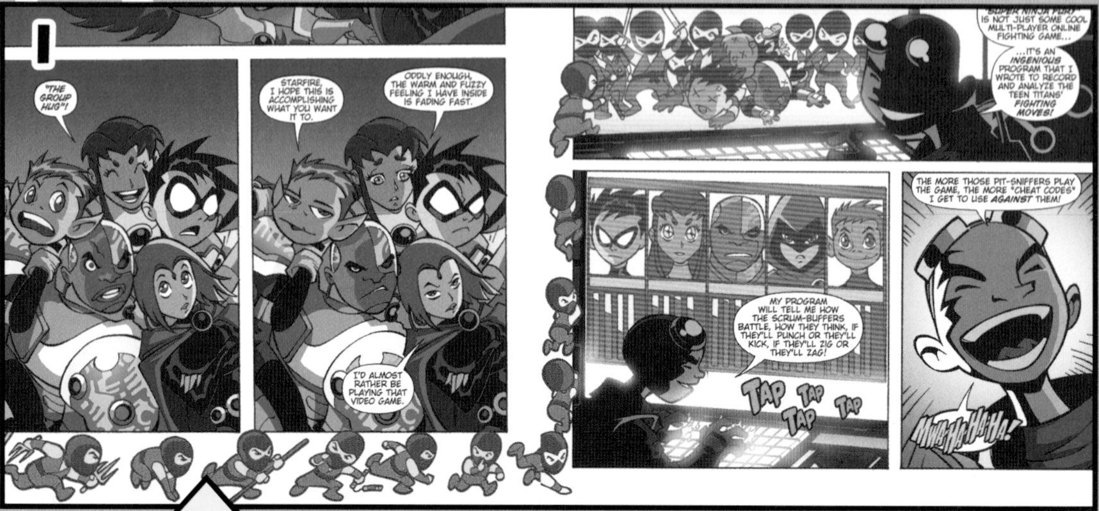

"THE GROUP HUG"!
STARFIRE, I HOPE THIS IS ACCOMPLISHING WHAT YOU WANT IT TO.
ODDLY ENOUGH, THE WARM AND FUZZY FEELING I HAVE INSIDE IS FADING FAST.
I'D ALMOST RATHER BE PLAYING THAT VIDEO GAME.
IS NOT JUST SOME COOL MULTI-PLAYER ONLINE FIGHTING GAME...
...IT'S AN INGENIOUS PROGRAM THAT I WROTE TO RECORD AND ANALYZE THE TEEN TITANS' FIGHTING MOVES!
MY PROGRAM WILL TELL ME HOW THE SCRUM-BUFFERS BATTLE, HOW THEY THINK, IF THEY'LL PUNCH OR THEY'LL KICK, IF THEY'LL ZIG OR THEY'LL ZAG!
TAP TAP TAP TAP
THE MORE THOSE PIT-SNIFFERS PLAY THE GAME, THE MORE "CHEAT CODES" I GET TO USE AGAINST THEM!
MWA-HA-HA-HA!

1. On page 12, we see little ninjas running across the panel border, up the gutter, and into another panel on page 13. Why do you think this comic's creators did this? Explain your answer.

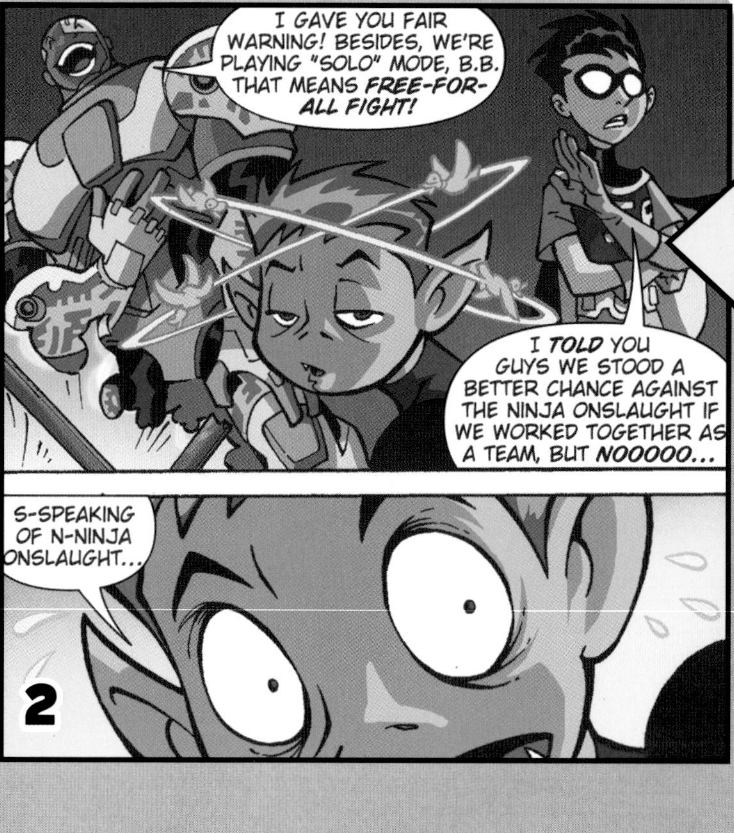

I GAVE YOU FAIR WARNING! BESIDES, WE'RE PLAYING "SOLO" MODE, B.B. THAT MEANS FREE-FOR-ALL FIGHT!
I TOLD YOU GUYS WE STOOD A BETTER CHANCE AGAINST THE NINJA ONSLAUGHT IF WE WORKED TOGETHER AS A TEAM, BUT NOOOOO...
S-SPEAKING OF N-NINJA ONSLAUGHT...

2. In the first panel, we see Beast Boy with birds flying around his head. In the second panel, we see drops of water dripping from his head. Based on these two facts, explain what you think Beast Boy is feeling in each panel. Reread page 10 if you need a hint.

3. Reread pages 8-11. What is the cause of confusion between Cyborg, Beast Boy, and Robin in these two panels? Explain.

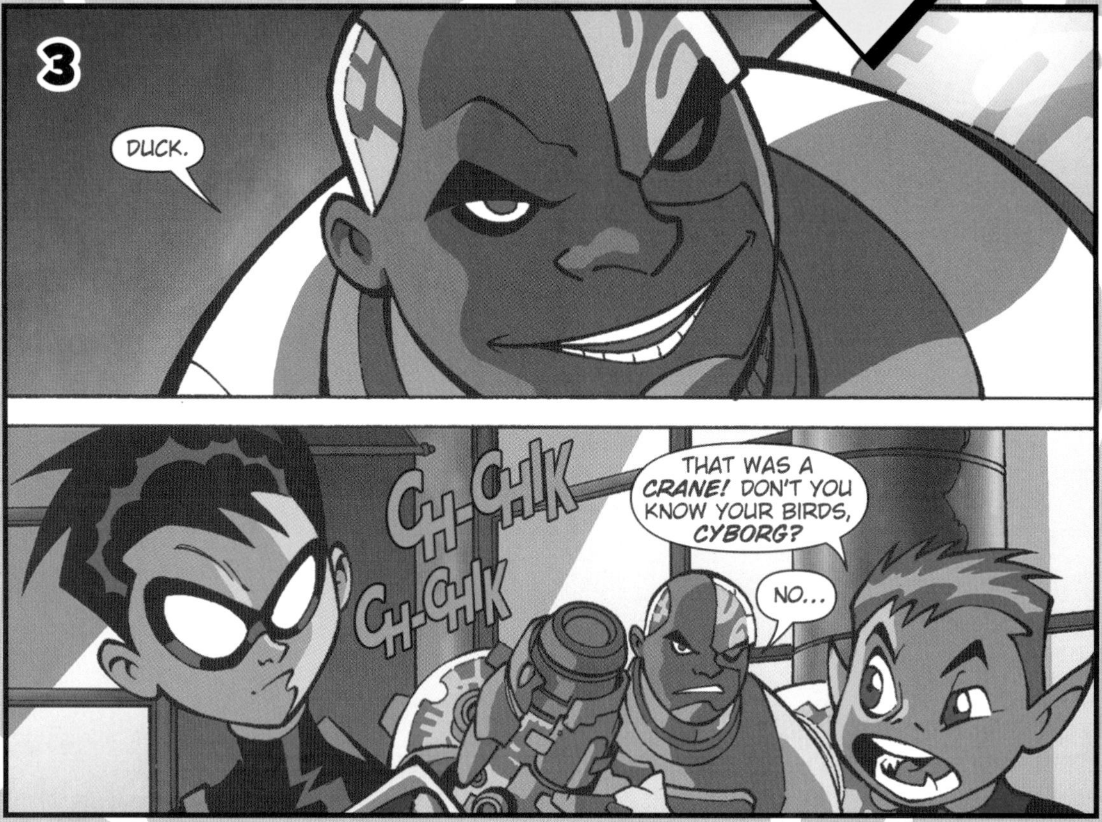
3
DUCK.
CH-CHIK
CH-CHIK
THAT WAS A CRANE! DON'T YOU KNOW YOUR BIRDS, CYBORG?
NO...

4. In this panel, both Robin and Beast Boy use the same martial arts skill. Which super hero would you rather be, and why?

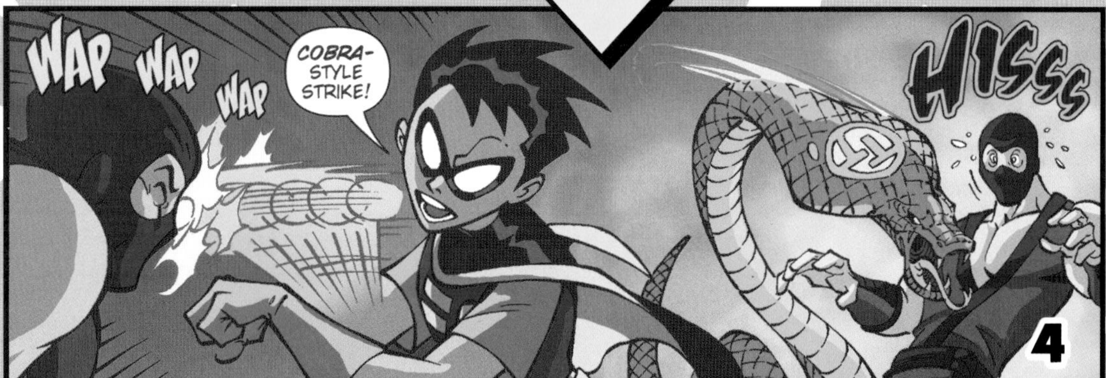
WAP WAP WAP
COBRA-STYLE STRIKE!
HISSS
4

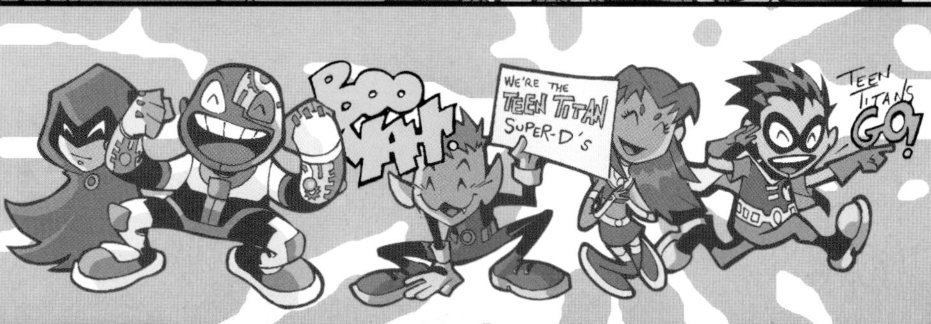
BOO YAH!
WE'RE THE TEEN TITAN SUPER-D'S
TEEN TITANS GO!

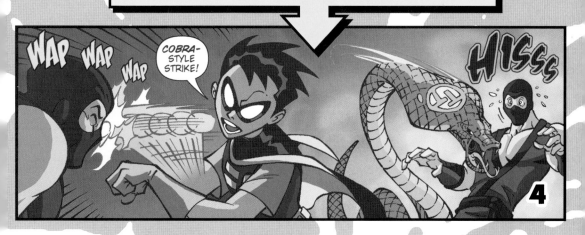

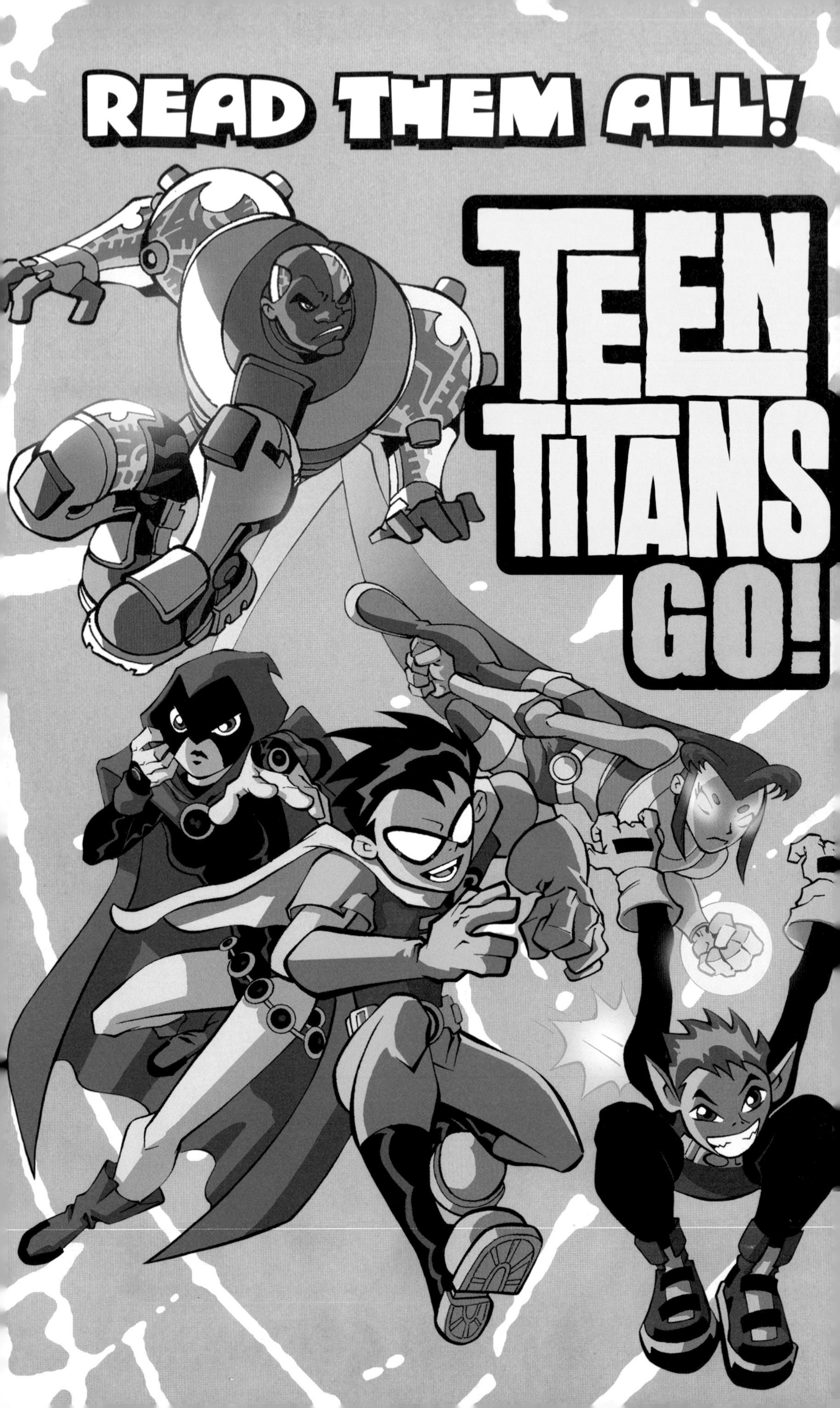
READ THEM ALL!
TEEN TITANS GO!

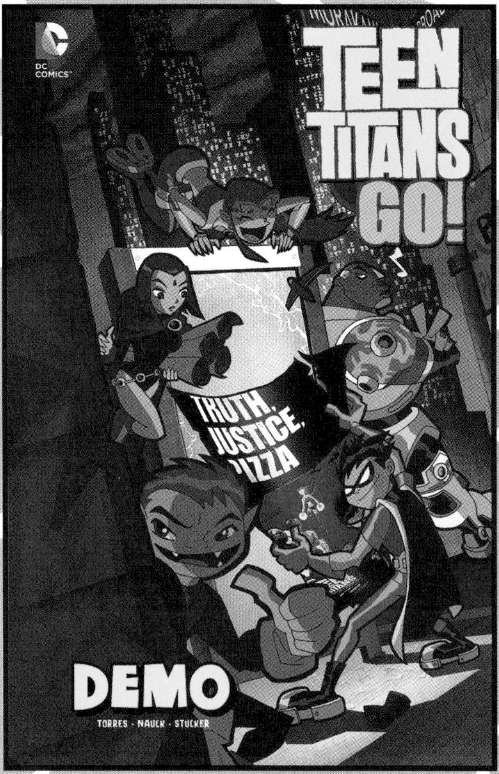
DC COMICS
TEEN TITANS GO!
TRUTH, JUSTICE, PIZZA
DEMO
TORRES · NAUCK · STUCKER

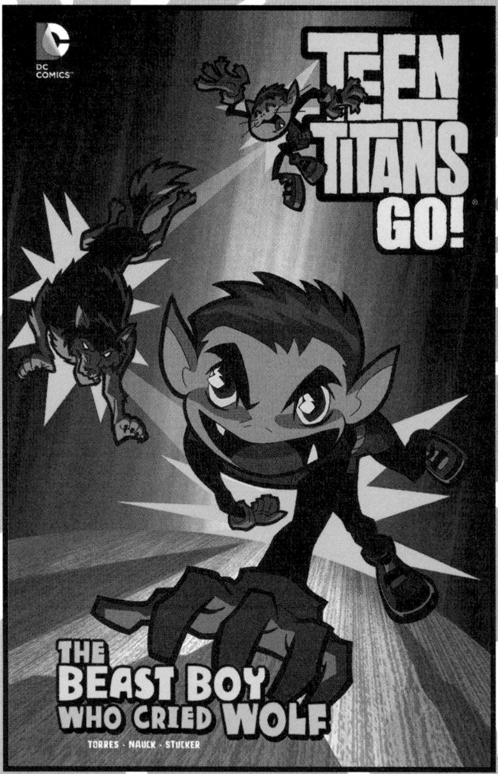
DC COMICS
TEEN TITANS GO!
THE BEAST BOY WHO CRIED WOLF
TORRES · NAUCK · STUCKER

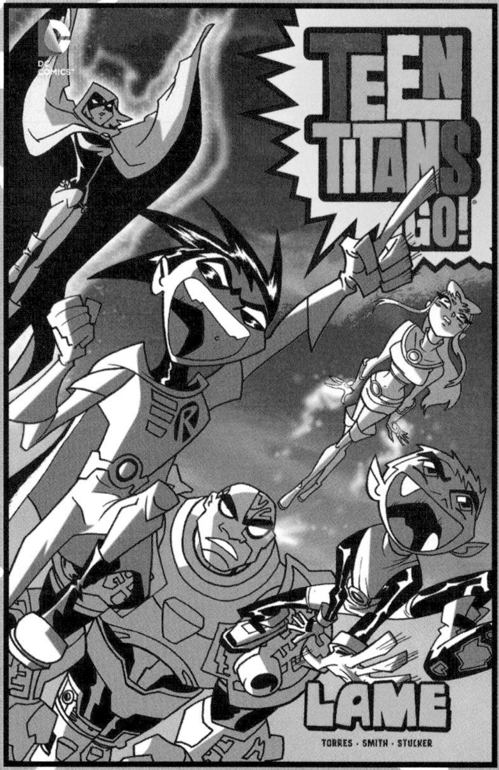
DC COMICS
TEEN TITANS GO!
LAME
TORRES · SMITH · STUCKER

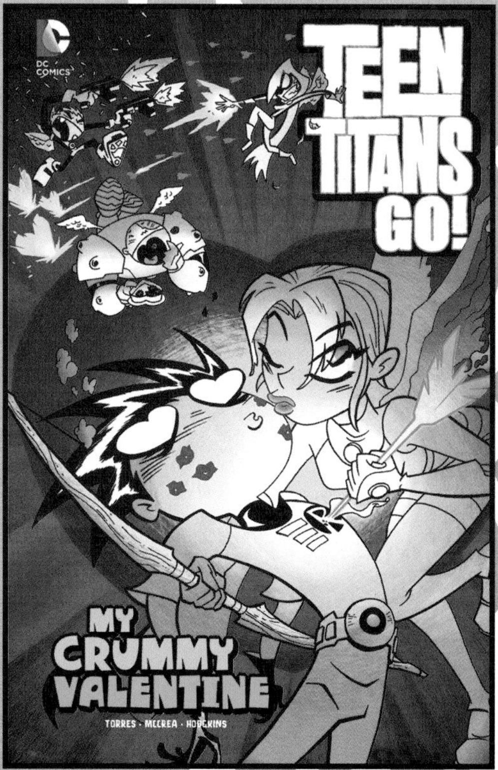
DC COMICS
TEEN TITANS GO!
MY CRUMMY VALENTINE
TORRES · MCCREA · HODGKINS

TEEN
TITANS
GO!®

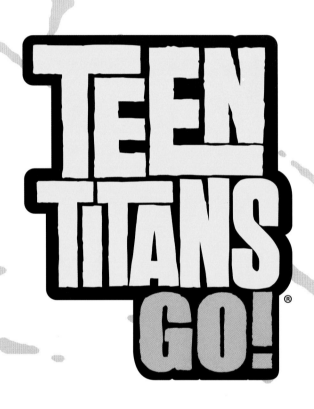